I0548377

The Second Book of THE MODERATOR

Coma

DWIGHT KOPP

The Coma - Copyright © 2013 Dwight Kopp

ISBN 978-0989585347

Cover Image Power Button © MS Media

All rights reserved. No part of this book may be reproduced or transmitted in any form or by any means, electronic or mechanical, including photocopying, recording, or any information storage and retrieval system, without prior written permission of the author.

All characters in this novel are fictitious. Any resemblance to actual persons—living or dead—is purely coincidental. All characters and situations are products of the author's imagination.

For Doe

Prolog

Beth Mallory hadn't done drugs until Solly introduced her. He found Beth hanging around the back of his store with a couple of boys her own age, trying to smoke a cigarette and pretending to act casual about it. He shooed the boys, sat down on the steps next to the thirteen-year-old, and introduced her to the great escape.

It didn't matter that Solly was twenty five years older than Beth. She needed weed to escape, and she needed Solly to get her the weed. It all worked out well for Solly until the girl started growing round. He blamed her for getting knocked up to the trailer trash, but she pouted and swore and eventually it was too late to do anything about it.

Social workers demanded paternity tests which Solly passed. Or failed. However Solly looked at it, the boy, Seth, was his.

Thankfully, Beth's mother, Ethel Maude Mallory, didn't want to press charges and the social worker didn't want to have to deal with a baby. Ethel Mallory was a stable fixture in the trailer park. That is to say, she hadn't moved in the last decade and most of her bills were up to date. Because of Ethel, Beth qualified as a fit mother and the overworked, underappreciated social worker was happy to leave well-enough alone; let the poor white trash work out their own social issues. Beth kept the baby. The social worker continued to bill the county for the case, but she spent most of her time in a coffee shop in nearby Trent, playing with her phone, getting fat on the pastries, and making up fiction to include in her case notes.

Ethel Maude Mallory never spoke with Solly about Seth. She didn't have the energy to keep after her daughter anymore, and she figured it was Beth's own damn fault for not keeping her legs together.

Ethel still came into Solly's grocery every month to cash out her social security check, buy a carton of menthol cigarettes, and play the lottery. Ethel didn't believe in banks. What little cash she had left over always went into a tidy bundle stored in a sealed bag under the newspaper in the parakeet cage. The parakeet had been dead for ages, but Ethel never cleaned the cage, and no one ever bothered the cash.

Chapter 1
18 Years Later

You want to play a game? Cold black words cut across the screen. The impatient cursor blinked. Don't keep The Moderator waiting. Hesitate too long, and he'll be gone.

This was no ordinary game.

Yes. He typed the word with one finger. Deliberately. He'd already set the necessary securities. TOR, The Onion Router offered him a chance to be invisible online.

Screen name *AMPED* already knew the rules.

Never talk about the game.
Play off line.
Win.

He got the game paper from someone on the track team, but they'd never spoken about it since. For his part, AMPED was thrilled to move beyond the silly nonsense of virtual gun fighting, virtual conquest, virtual robbery.

Now it was his turn to be untraceable, powerful and dangerous.

The game was narcotic.

Chapter 2

Chase Hikeman wasn't sure what door to use. The too-clean, faux-marble walkway made Chase feel like he needed to wash his hands and trim his fingernails. Automatic sprinklers rose like hissing black mushrooms from the putting-green lawn.

Who waters their lawn in the fall? Chase wondered.

The oak front door squared off against visitors with a pretentious, uninviting, never-used look. Rich, clean and sterile. Chase shook his head. He needed to talk to Darren.

Darren Firth was everything Chase wasn't: tall, strong, and athletic. He led the high school swim team which some people whispered was heading to nationals this year. Darren stood comfortably around six feet with shoulders that telegraphed a subtle don't-mess-with-me to anyone foolish enough to consider otherwise.

Chase smoothed down his churlish coffee hair and knocked on the oak. The wood swallowed the sound. A stone gargoyle glared from its perch beside the door. Chase knocked again. Louder.

He left the porch and cut across the grass. The sprinklers hissed all over his legs. Chase cupped his hands to peek through the curtained side-window of an attached three car garage with medieval doors. Utility shelves lined the far wall and a green riding mower sat alongside. The garage floor sported too-clean concrete and no cars.

He heard something at the front door and dodged the sprinklers on his way back.

Darren saw him and leaned into the open doorway. "Hey."

Chase felt weird. It wasn't like they never saw each other in school, but Chase and Darren might as well have lived in different countries. "Hey. Do you have a minute?"

"Sure. Wanna come in?"

Chase followed Darren into the living room. A bronze, Chinese dragon dominated a black coffee table. Its forked tongue lolled from the side of its mouth. Chase stopped to look at it. A lion's mane radiated back from its head and eagle-like talons reached toward the front door.

"Someone born the year of the dragon?" Chase asked.

"My mom. Kind of welcoming, isn't it?"

Chase touched the bridge of his glasses to settle them on his nose. "Does she have the dragon attributes?"

Darren was surprised at Chase's interest. "Yes, I suppose: She's controlling, artistic, and mean as hell." He sprawled on the brown leather sofa. "This about Lisa?" he asked.

"Sort of." Chase sat on an opposing chair.

"I figured someone would come by eventually." Darren looked over at Chase. "I just didn't expect it to be you."

"You weren't at the funeral." Chase stated the obvious. Not an accusation.

"No. We broke up, remember?"

"But you were still friends, right?"

Darren sat up and stared at the carpeted floor. "Yeah, sure."

"You want to talk about what happened?" Chase asked.

Darren's face twisted at the memory, then resolved. "You here because of the hate mail?"

"No," Chase replied, then added, "And yes." Ashley had told him about the letters. Only one of them had names attached. It had been signed by every member of the swim team. Only one name was missing. Darren's. "Ashley has the papers, but I don't think anyone else has seen them. She hid them because she didn't want all the hoopla of a big investigation. Mostly, she didn't want the world to know that her sister... well, you know." Chase didn't finish.

"What is she going to do with them?" Darren asked.

"Destroy them, I think," Chase said. "I told her to keep them for a bit. I'm trying to figure something out. Can you tell me why all those guys signed that card?" The card had an elementary kind of look to it. Childish letters scrawled across the middle read, *'you'll make the world a better place, when you leave it.'*

"It was my idea." Darren's voice was flat. "The guys didn't know what the card would say. They just signed the paper. I filled it in later."

"Your idea? I thought you loved Lisa." Chase's eyes narrowed.

"Love? No. Not really. It started as a game." Darren shook his head and added. "Then it got out of hand."

"What do you mean?"

"It's complicated."

"Try me. I'm smart."

6

"Why should I tell you?" Darren asked.

"Because, I'm guessing you haven't told anyone else." Chase studied the senior. "Some secrets are like splinters."

"Splinters?"

"Yes. They feel better once they're out."

Chapter 3

Sonya Hernandez wore her spider girl costume. Silver on black. Even her nails matched. The Courthouse Crime Records Department unofficially called the party and most of the paralegals came. A few of the local police departments were invited as well. After all, what was a party without a few guys?

Annie Bailey's Irish Pub on Halloween felt like a movie set. Masks and capes and fish net stockings lent an ethereal, almost ghost-like feel to the worn teak flooring and black bar stools. Even the bartender, a stocky, bald man with an honest-to-God, Maori tattoo on his face, fit in. He once played professional rugby and somehow ended up here, tending bar. Today he blended in. On a normal day Tama and his tattoo were considered part of the pub's decoration.

"Hey, Tama." Sonya put her hands on the bar so he'd notice the silver webs on her nails. "Can I get a red martini?" It would look great with the black spandex, she thought.

"Sure. Want me to start you a tab?"

"Of course, unless you're buying," she gave him a flirty wink.

"Sorry. Not today. Got to buy food for the kids, you know?"

"Sure, Tama. Whatever."

He mixed up schnapps and vodka and added a splash of cranberry juice before handing her the glass and a napkin. "Thanks mate," she said.

He gave her a little grin and the tattoo on his chin spread out. She liked it. It suited him.

Sonya headed toward the back where the rest of the paralegals assembled to compare outfits and swap stories.

"What are you?" She poked one finger into the flannel shirt of Officer Ken Dixon.

"Cowboy." He spread his arms so she could get a better look. Jeans under a large silver buckle. Snake skin boots.

"How original. Let me guess; you forgot about the party until this afternoon?"

"Maybe."

"Where are your spurs?"

"Tama made me leave them at the door. Didn't want me to scratch up the floor."

"Sure he did." Sonya put a hand on her hip. "Good thing you're kinda cute, or we'd have to ask you to leave. This is a costume-only party."

Another woman slipped up beside Sonya and gave her a hip bump.

"Hey, girl." Lucy wore the red version of Sonya's outfit. They shopped together. Of course, Lucy looked great.

"Take a picture for us?" Sonya handed the phone to Ken without waiting for an answer. Ken put his beer on a table, framed them up with her phone and touched the screen. Red and black. Quite a pair.

"Perfect. Want a full body shot?" he asked.

"Whatever you want," Lucy said. Her rum and coke was already working.

"You going to update your page with that?" Ken Dixon handed Sonya the phone.

"Probably, but my laptop crapped out, and I hate trying to do real work on my phone."

"That sucks. Maybe Farwick can fix it for you."

"Who's Farwick?"

"Our cyber detective. Really good at all that techie stuff. Even works with other departments sometimes. Maybe you can sweet talk him into helping you. Come, I'll introduce you."

Dixon led the way through a cluster of winged fairies to a booth. A black man with a yellow and green Rastafarian wig sat drinking something golden from a short glass. Thick twisted locks hung over his shoulders.

"Farwick, I found a damsel in distress. This is Sonya Hernandez. She works as a paralegal over at the Crime Records Department."

Farwick peered over the top of his Stevie Wonder sunglasses to get a better look.

Dixon continued, "She said her computer is on the blink. Thought maybe you could buy her a drink and fix her up."

"Those dreads real?" Sonya slipped into his booth.

"Only today," he replied. "Ready for another drink?"

She flicked her web-covered nails on the glass. "Only if you can help me."
Preston Farwick smiled. "Deal."

10

Chapter 4

"It was just supposed to be a game." Ashley shrugged, miserable.

Something arced in Chase's mind. This was way too coincidental. "What game?"

"The game I was playing that got me *in trouble*." Her tone carried a distinct 'no-duh.'

"That all you can tell me?"

"I don't know," Ashley's face started getting blotchy. It always happened just before she cried.

"You don't know or you don't want to tell me?" Chase pressed.

Ashley was scared. "I'm not allowed to talk about it."

"Why not? Did your dad tell you that?"

"No."

"Who then?"

"He did."

"He who?" Chase tried to be patient.

"The one who set up the game," Ashley said.

"So how could he find out?" Chase asked.

"I don't know, but he always does."

A creepy something crawled up the back of Chase's neck. "So what happens if he finds out?"

Ashley whispered, "I'll be in trouble."

"What kind of trouble?" Chase kept fishing.

She moved a little closer; he didn't mind that. She bit her lip then went on, "My mother has, or had—I'm not sure—mental issues."

"So? Who cares? What does that have to do with anything?" Chase asked, unfazed.

"He threatened to spread it around if I talk about the game," she said.

"He blackmailed you?"

"I guess. Sort of."

"You guess?" Chase couldn't believe it. "This guy have a name?"

She tucked a loose strand of hair behind her ear and lowered her voice. "We call him The Moderator."

Chase was on his feet. "Holy shit."

Chapter 5

Solly Gamber's market had squared off against the new franchise convenience mart and gas station across the street. For all intents and purposes, Solly's Mart was losing badly. It boasted an awkward mix of dollar hot dogs, fishing worms and cigarettes. The better employees crossed the street early on to find a kinder place to work, where the linoleum wasn't peeling off the floor and they could get a little more money for their time.

The employees who stayed behind couldn't pass another drug test or were somehow related to the owner.

Seth Mallory was both. He fell into the category of 'somehow' related, though everyone knew him as Solly's Bastard. A few even called him that to his face. Seth pretended not to care. He lived his life from paycheck to paycheck so he could throw a few bucks at the social worker to leave him alone and hand the rest over to Solly's supplier. Seth wasn't just Solly's Bastard, he was an addict, just like his mother. He didn't do the hard stuff, but he needed marijuana to keep himself sane, sober and employable.

Besides, Seth figured his music was better when he smoked a little weed.

On the weekends, Seth would leave Morris and head over to his cousin's house in Trent. Not only did Nick have a garage that was clean enough for them to practice, but the house was a bomb. Seth wasn't exactly sure what Nick's parents did for a living. He didn't pay much attention to that. But Seth did notice the pool, and the cute girls that hung around to listen to their latest licks. And it gave him the chance to get away from his way-too-young mother.

Not that there was anything else to do in Morris. His town was nothing more than a poor excuse for a truck-stop wedged somewhere between the affluent neighborhoods and the river. Only Morris was closer to the river. Its claims to fame were its unsavory history as a river town and the worst school district in the entire county. Not only were the kids bad, but they were—at least according to the state assessments—well below average.

Seth's own mother was a product of the trailer park scattered up along the hill. It bordered a Texan-owned natural gas transfer station that blew off pressure and filled the air with its foul-smelling discharge. No one ever complained. It was farm country, after all. Rare country air was a given.

Chapter 6

The day she won, Ethel Mallory was standing in line behind a man with a yellow fishing license pinned to his hat. She'd waited while he fished around in his pocket for a missing quarter. A quarter he needed to pay for the Canadian night-crawlers and his one dollar lottery ticket. She smiled and leaned hard on her three-toed cane and eventually, he let her go in front.

Ethel pulled the winning ticket. $100,000 after taxes.

Solly's Mart was an instant local sensation. For a week, lines from the register wrapped around the sticky soda island and out the side door.

Solly got rich, but Ethel Maude Mallory was richer.

Chapter 7

Nick Rail tuned up his bass and sat down on the amplifier to play. Lana Summers curled on a lawn chair by the open garage door sucking on a juice pop. Fall served up something of an Indian summer, but the evening stole its warmth.

"Ten bucks says he'll bitch about his mother before he starts playing," Lana said.

"Leave him alone. Have you ever met her?" Nick asked.

"No."

"She's everything he says she is."

"What do you mean?"

"Definitely a co-dependent, immature, major pain in the ass." Nick followed up with a bass riff for emphasis.

"What does she do?"

"Beth, do?" Nick scowled. "Absolutely nothing she doesn't want. She sometimes lives at home with her mother. She probably hasn't cooked Seth a meal in his entire life."

"No shit." Lana thought about that.

Seth played a blues line nice and slow, closed his eyes and felt the vibration in his pants.

Lana stood next to him, and put her icy hand on his shoulder. "I wish we could do something for him."

"Well, at least he can come here. I don't know what he likes more. Playing guitar, getting away from his mother, or seeing you."

"What are you talking about?"

"Come on. You know he can't take his eyes off you."

Lana made a face. "You sound jealous."

"Nope. I'm the one with the girl. But if he didn't play guitar, I wouldn't let him come."

"He is a pretty good guitar player," Lana offered.

"Sure. He's not bad."

"Where is he, anyway?" she asked.

"He said he had to work today, but I thought he'd be here by now."

A car pulled to a stop out front. Seth came kicking up the drive, guitar in tow and the car pulled away.

"We were just about to give up on you," Nick said.

"Sorry. Solly made me work late. Crazy at the shop, you know."

"What, some kind of sale on burnt coffee?"

"Very funny. Didn't you hear?"

"Hear what?"

"I thought everyone had heard. Granny won the lottery, and Solly's Mart is now the lucky charm."

"Your grandma?" Lana asked.

"One and the same." Seth unzipped the guitar's fabric case and threw it on the garage floor.

"Wait a minute. You mean your grandmother is a millionaire?" Nick asked.

"Nah. News says she only took home a hundred grand."

"Cool." Lana squeezed on the amp next to her boyfriend. "You gonna see any of that?"

"Hell, no." Seth seemed surprised by the idea.

"Really?" Lana was shocked.

"Not a dime. She's as tight as my mother is loose." Seth reached into his pocket and pulled out a joint. His lighter flashed and the end caught. He plugged in, set the distortion, and let his fingers roll over the frets making loud, angry music.

Chapter 8

Music swirled over the sound of the rock fountain and mingled with the ferns. The deep brown and black leather tone of the office seemed to hold the falling music of Chopin and water in some other place, as if someone were playing in another room.

Here and there, The Moderator's voice, a deep melodic bass, joined the piano floating from the speakers on his desk. He studied the response from username AMPED. He had a new player. A player more willing than the others.

This one needed little prodding.

The Moderator considered his response. He typed, *Are you just going to take it?*

AMPED returned quickly. *No. I'm going to kill her first.*

Chapter 9

Preston Farwick parallel parked and pulled the keys, checked his teeth in the rear view mirror before getting out. He scanned the doors and found Sonya's apartment number. He'd shed some weight since joining the Florin Police Department as their cyber detective. Over all, he felt good, but Sonya's twenty-seven-year-old body and Latina figure made him a bit self-conscious.

"Forget it, Farwick. She just wants you to fix her computer." Not that he minded. Some things in life just came too easy.

He shut the car door and climbed the stairs to her apartment. An iron knocker hung over peeling paint. He lifted the fob and let it drop.

Sonya opened the door. "Hi, Preston. Come in." Heels and pantyhose lay in a tangle by a wall mirror beneath a coat rack. "I was hoping you hadn't forgotten."

"Me? Forget?"

"Well, I wasn't sure how much you had to drink after we talked," Sonya said. "Of course, I don't remember how much I had to drink either. All I know is Saturday morning woke me with a headache I won't soon forget."

Farwick chuckled. "Sorry to hear that."

"The computer's over here." She led him through the living room to an antique secretary desk. A black wireless router sat incongruously on top.

"So what's the matter with it?" he asked.

"It isn't working," she replied helplessly. "I turn it on and all I get is a blank screen."

"May I?"

"Please do."

Farwick sat down in the office chair and pushed the power button. The startup began but blinked off. "BSOD," Farwick muttered.

Sonya spent a couple of seconds trying to figure out the acrostic. "BSOD?"

"Yep. Blue Screen of Death."

"Great. That sounds promising."

"Maybe, maybe not."

"What are the odds?" she asked.

"Fifty-fifty," he replied.

"Shit. That's not good."

"No. Not really. I'm probably going to have to take it with me. I'll need to hook it up to another hard drive and see if I can jump start it. That okay?"

"Yes. I mean if you don't mind."

"Not a problem." He picked up the laptop and power cord and headed back through the living room.

"Any idea what it's going to cost me?" Sonya opened the door for him.

21

Farwick heard the edge in her question. "Not sure. You might have to let me buy you another drink."

"That, I can do," Sonya smiled. "Name the time."

"I'll have to check with the wife first and let you know." He gave her a wink and walked out.

Chapter 10

Farwick set the laptop on his desk, restarted the computer in safe mode and restored it to a previously established reset date. He ran a couple of virus and malware programs to tidy up the problem and then got down to the real work.

Farwick made sure his own computer would clear her firewall and set up hers to allow remote desktop connection. In fifteen minutes, he'd finished. He would be able to access her computer, see her screen on his own while she was working, turn on her webcam and dig through all her files. All he needed was her router password. She must have purchased it since the reset date. Once he had that, she would be back on line and he would be in business.

Time to call it in.

He dialed her number.

Sonya picked up. "Hernandez."

"Sonya? It's Preston Farwick."

"Hi, Preston." Sonya's voice turned from business to pleasant. "How are you?"

"I'm fine. Wish I could say the same for your computer, however."

Sonya groaned on the other end. Farwick smiled.

"How bad is it?" she asked.

"Still figuring that out. Do you have a lot of pictures and stuff on there you're hoping to save?"

"Yes, all my pictures are there. New nephew, sister's wedding, She's going to flip out." Sonya went silent.

"I think your computer's security was compromised. Some kind of Trojan virus. We probably got it in time. That's the good news. Bad news is I have to replace the hard drive. I may still be able to retrieve your data, but I'm not sure yet. I'm afraid it is going to take me a little while."

Sonya swore. "Sounds expensive."

"Listen, don't worry about that. Unless you're in a rush, I'll just keep working at it when I have the time. Don't stress about the money."

"I don't know what to say."

"Say nothing. Are you at home now?" he asked.

"No. Not yet. I had to work late."

"Fine. Well, I'm going to have to reconfigure your router, so you'll have to text me the password. It's usually a 12-digit string. You still have the paperwork that came with it?"

"I think so. I'll call you as soon as I get home."

She thanked him again and hung up.

The Moderator locked his hands behind his head. "Sonya Hernandez, you are too easy."

Chapter 11

Chase Hikeman sat on the church stairs. His knuckles were cracked and dry, but they did that every Fall. He sniffed and shivered and waited.

They hadn't talked much since the funeral. Ashley did some community service and her dad—somehow—kept his job as a pastor. Chase didn't know how that worked. Ashley was certain Lisa's death would end all that. The church people wouldn't abide a pastor whose daughter committed suicide.

Ashley said she didn't want her dad to be unemployed, necessarily. Just that she wanted something else, and she didn't know what that was.

Chase wanted something, too. He wanted the old Ashley back. She hadn't been herself since Lisa died. But then, who would be? Nobody's sister is supposed to die like that. Maybe on the news, but not in your own house. The cold pushed up from the cement and Chase shifted.

Ashley appeared on the sidewalk. Her complexion favored the fall. Blond hair and fair skin worked well with the corduroy jacket and jeans. Her sad green eyes didn't look like they belonged to a kid anymore.

"You're late," he said dusting off his butt.

"Where are we going?" she asked.

"You'll see." Chase wasn't sure why she bothered with him. She stood several inches taller. In high school, that seemed to matter. He didn't care, but *people* cared, whoever they were.

She fell in beside him. Ashley always smelled a little like sandalwood.

"What's this all about?" Her hands rode deep in her pockets. Maybe she was afraid he would make a pass at her.

But he knew she wasn't interested. Besides, he had something else on his mind.

"I want you to meet someone."

"Who? I don't feel like meeting anyone."

"Come on. This is important."

"You always say that."

"Only if it's true."

"I have homework," she said.

It was true. Since her sister died, Ashley had become a student. A real student. Chase cared about learning too, only not the stuff they force fed him at school. Ashley studied to get away. She studied to hide from the world and maybe from herself.

"This is more important than homework," Chase grabbed her arm. "Come on."

Chapter 12

Lana rummaged for earrings, the little black spikes she got to match her hair. What she really wanted was an eyebrow piercing, but her mom wasn't there yet. Maybe she could talk her into it for Christmas. What single parent could deny that?

Lana buttoned up her shirt and picked at her new hairdo. Her mom finally consented to the black dye with red and white highlights. Lana had to promise she wasn't going over to the 'dark side.' Nick was going to like it. She and Nick had been steady for quite a while. His parents were cool and sometimes they would hang out at his house. They almost never hung out at her place.

Her mother took the hovering-parent thing to a whole new level. When Nick was there, Lana's mother would want to play board games or watch movies with them. Way old school. Not a great recipe for making out.

Tonight they had a date. Officially, she and Nick were 'going out with friends.' At least that was how she put it to her mother. It kept her mom from asking awkward questions. Lana used her teeth to open the too-tight lid on the liquid eyeliner and leaned against the mirror to draw it on. It smelled funny and made her blue eyes burn. She flirted a black swoosh into the corners. Nick noticed the little things. That's one of the reasons she liked him. He always made her feel special. Something her ex-dad had long ago forgotten how to do.

She backed up, studied herself and teased open another button to show a little more lace. Nick would like that, too.

Lana heard the growl of Nick's car turning into their drive, and she bolted from the room.

"My ride's here, Mom," Lana called.

Her mother was on the phone, and Lana didn't wait for a reply.

Chapter 13

Ashley followed Chase until they stood in front of Darren Firth's house.

"Chase. I'm not ready for this." Darren had been Lisa's boyfriend.

"Ready for what?"

"Ready to talk to Darren."

"Humor me," Chase led her through the empty garage and opened the inside door.   The kitchen gleamed with stainless steel and polished cherry cabinets.

Chase walked in like he lived there. They crossed to a basement door. Carpeted stairs led them past a fully stocked bar. It didn't feel like a basement. Soft recessed lights illuminated the space. Burnt ochre walls curved around a family room that looked like it had never been used. A tree, made entirely of twisted silver wire, reached out from between two upholstered armchairs. An abstract mosaic design of black glass and turquoise stone had been tiled into a circle on the wall.

"Wow," Ashley said, temporarily distracted.

"I thought you'd been here before," Chase said.

"No. Why would I have been here?"

Chase shrugged and led her past the living room toward the back of the basement. A for-real sliding book shelf opened to a secret library. The only basement room with no windows.   Chase whispered, "Darren's mom is an interior architect."

Ashley stepped into the room and Chase slid the bookshelf back into place behind them. She backed up against the bookshelves, awkward and uncomfortable.

"Hey, Darren," Chase said.

Darren Firth got up and came to her. She couldn't look at him. She didn't know what part he had played in bullying her sister. Chase decided to clean his glasses.

Darren put a hand on her shoulder, but she shrugged it off. "I don't want to be here," she said. It was a whisper.

"I don't, either," Darren said. "But you and I have something in common."

"I don't have anything in common with you." Ashley glared at him. She expected to see eyes as hard and cold as her own.

Instead, tears rolled unfettered down his face. She softened. "I'm sorry."

"No. You're right. You have reason to hate me. But we do share something. We've both played games that hurt other people, and we've both been blackmailed."

"What are you talking about?" Ashley tried to sneer, but it wasn't convincing.

"The Moderator," Darren replied.

Ashley lifted her head; her eyes locked with Darren's. The sound of the name shook Ashley.

"I think we need to talk," Darren mashed tears off his face.

Ashley's lip quivered a bit, but she nodded. "Okay."

Chapter 14

Nick turned down a long gravel road that led to an abandoned quarry filled with water. The lane turned at a grove of trees and ended abruptly. Nick had found an old basket and talked his mom into packing something interesting for supper. He rummaged through the attic steamer trunk and found a couple of quilts his grandmother patched together. It would probably be the last good picnic weather of the year.

"The almost-punk look suits you," Nick said.

"You like it?" Lana smiled.

"Hell, yeah." Nick gave her leg a squeeze.

Lana made the varsity cheer squad in her sophomore year. Nick noticed her first when he was running track. They started going out soon after, but Nick dropped track because he wanted to spend more time in his garage practicing with Seth Mallory and Pete Finnerty. Lana seemed to like hanging out at his parent's place, which suited Nick. She was hot when she danced, and she liked their music.

Nick unfastened the snaps on the car top so he could put it down. A little starlight would be romantic.

"Come on back." He pointed to the back seat. "I'll get you a blanket."

He produced the blanket and picnic basket and climbed in to snuggle beside her.

"It's hard to believe Seth's grandmother has all that money and lives in such a rotten little hole in the ground." Lana hadn't brought up the money since their last practice.

"I know, but she's lived that way as long as I can remember. It's like some people just don't know how to be wealthy. At least, that's what my dad says."

"So how is it that you guys hang together? I mean, your parents are rich, at least compared to Seth."

"I dunno. I guess my folks feel a little sorry for Seth. After all, his mom is my aunt, even if she is a waste. Ever since we started playing guitar together, I guess we just kinda clicked. My folks didn't want me hanging out over there, so they cleared the garage for us." Nick put Lana's legs up over his own and pulled the quilt tighter around them.

"You ever been here before?" he asked.

"I didn't know the place existed."

"Nor does anyone else."

Chapter 15

Jesús Santiago pulled his cell from jeans sagging well south of his silver boxers. He wore a crisp white wife-beater and a thick silver chain with a crucifix. "Hey?" He pressed the phone against his ear and squinted into the smoke coming off the grill.

Jesús listened for a while then pulled a toothpick from his mouth and threw it into the grass. "You want what? What do you need that for?"

The caller hesitated then explained. Jesús fingered the crucifix around his neck. "Listen, I didn't hear that. I don't want to know that shit. Who gave you this number?"

Jesús lifted the grill cover and carefully flipped the hamburgers, squinting again for the smoke and heat.

"Damn. You're crazy. She's how old?"

The burgers spat hot fat that sizzled on the flame diffuser below.

Jesús closed the grill. "Shit, man. All you need is a baseball bat or a hammer, but I'll see what I can do."

He pushed a button and shoved the phone back into his pocket.

Chapter 16

AMPED logged in and waited.

Black words materialized on the screen. *You ready?*

Yes, and I'm taking a friend.

Sounds like a d8.

Kind of. LOL.

Good. Who's paying?

They are.

Chapter 17

Darren Firth brewed coffee but Ashley turned it down, even after he offered to spike it up a little.

"Are your parents ever home?" Ashley asked.

"Nah, thank God. I see them some on weekends."

Chase Hikeman had some plan he wanted them to hear about, but he hadn't arrived yet. It felt a little weird, sitting alone with Darren in an empty house. Antique maps decorated the library walls, and old books loaded down the shelves. It reminded Ashley of her dad's library.

"You read a lot?" she asked.

"No. My mom bought all those at an auction because she thought they'd look good on the shelf. Just for show, you know."

Darren crossed a leg underneath and settled into the wingback with his coffee. "You wanna sit?"

She picked the chair opposite. Ashley still didn't know what to think of him.

"I need to tell you something," he said.

"Okay." I'll humor him, she thought.

He struggled with it for a bit, then said, simply. "I'm gay."

Ashley couldn't speak. Didn't know what to say. At last she managed an, "Oh."

But Darren wasn't finished. "That's what The Moderator held over me. I thought if I broke up with Lisa, then he'd leave me alone about it."

"I see." She didn't really. It was a bit much to take in.

The sliding door opened and Chase came in with two other boys. One he introduced as Ralph; the other was Nick.

Ralph looked around the office and smiled. "Sweet."

Where did Chase find this guy? Ralph looked like someone who would be comfortable on his back, knuckle deep in the engine of someone's car. Black skinny jeans, a wallet chain and a raid-the-fridge feel about him. His clean hands surprised her. So did the body odor. Green fingernail polish covered three nails on each hand. Black on the others.

Nick looked like Ralph's opposite. Where Ralph's hair crazed about in wild curls, Nick's hung straight, partially overhanging one eye. Nick's jeans had a store-bought grunge look about them, and he was cute.

Chase got things started. "Nick passed his game paper to his cousin and gave an extra to Darren. Darren passed one to Ashley. Nick said he wanted to help out if he could."

"Hey," Nick nodded to the group.

Chase continued. "This is Ralph. He's going to help us track down The Moderator."

#

The five teenagers huddled in the library of the otherwise empty house and listened to the plan.

"It's all about triangulation," Ralph said.

Ashley rolled her eyes. "Chase. Make him speak English. Just because you understand doesn't mean the rest of us can."

"Explain it, Ralph," Chase said.

"Right." Ralph grabbed paper from a printer in the corner. He knelt by the coffee table and drew three intersecting circles. "These circles represent interactions with The Moderator. Where they intersect forms a much smaller area and gets us much closer."

"How does that help us find him?" Darren asked.

"Simple, really," said Ralph. "Every interaction helps to locate the bad guy. The more interactions we get, the greater the likelihood we'll find him."

"How is that supposed to work? Everyone who played with him used an onion router. He's invisible," Ashley said.

"Yes, his IP address is invisible, but he's still giving himself away. Chase thinks The Moderator might live in this area."

"How do you figure?" Darren asked.

"Well, there are several clues. First of all, The Moderator knew things you didn't tell him. He seemed to know about your neighborhood. He said he'll know if you 'talk' to anyone. The whole premise of his game is that it is played offline. That's another clue. He probably 'plays' offline as well."

"Seems like a weak link to me," Ashley wasn't buying.

"It is, so far," Chase admitted. "But Ralph thinks we can find other gamers and triangulate from them."

"How are you going to do that? Everything they do is hidden online. It's all anonymous," she said.

Nick jumped in. "Chase told me The Moderator usually challenges kids to do something illegal, right?"

Ashley bit her lip and nodded.

Nick continued, "Good. That makes it easy. We'll just look up all the kids in the county who committed a crime that was connected to some kind of online game. The more hits we get, the closer we are to finding the common thread."

"Sounds like a longshot," Darren said.

"It isn't going to work," Ashley flopped back in her chair.

"Why?" Ralph asked.

"Because all the juvenile records are confidential," she said, "No one except the kid's parents are allowed to look at them. They're not going to let us walk in and start pulling files."

"True. Almost," Chase said.

"What do you mean, 'almost'?" she asked.

"The courts are allowed to access those records," Chase replied.

"And how does that help us?" Ashley was getting impatient.

"It helps Ralph," Chase said.

"How?" Darren wasn't tracking either.

Chase fingered his glasses into place. "Because Ralph is a hacker."

They dropped into silence.

Darren spoke up. "So you're suggesting we, I mean he, hack into the county court and pull all the records for kids who've been targeted by The Moderator, in hopes of finding the magic link."

Ashley stood up. "I think you're crazy. Even if you could hack in there, I don't think you're going to find anything."

"How do you know?" Chase asked.

"Chase, this is a job for the police. Not something for a few nerds, a gay swimmer — sorry Darren — and a pastor's daughter. I'm in enough trouble already."

"And what have the police turned up so far?" Ralph asked.

"Nothing," Ashley admitted.

"You do realize," said Ralph, "that if the police don't do anything, and we don't do anything then The Moderator can strike again, right?"

"That doesn't justify breaking into the courthouse and getting into everyone else's business," Ashley moved to leave.

"What do you think Lisa would want you to do?" Chase asked.

Ashley stopped and turned on Chase. "How dare you?" She locked eyes with him through thick lenses. "Listen to me, you little skank. Lisa's got nothing to do with your crazy scavenger hunt. And I'm going to have nothing to do with it either."

The hidden door slammed open and Ashley walked out.

Chase looked up at the ceiling. "I'm so stupid."

Chapter 18

Seth sat cross-legged on the living room floor. He picked up his electric guitar. He didn't have an amp and his grandmother would probably complain about it if he did. Without an amplifier, the notes sounded muted and flat. Nick and Lana had gone out and he had no ride and no place to get away. He wasn't even scheduled to work. Normally being home with his grandmother wasn't so bad, until his mother showed up.

Like tonight.

She never came alone. This guy didn't seem much older than Seth. They stumbled hand-in-hand, into the mobile home like they lived there. Which of course they didn't. At least his mother didn't very often. Officially Seth and his mother shared the second bedroom, but his mother was almost never there, thank God. When she was, Seth moved to the couch.

It was better that way.

Chapter 19

Sonya Hernandez pulled on Yoga pants and stretched out on the living room floor. It was getting colder and soon she'd be consigned to the gym and treadmills and lines of televisions. Not many running days left. She lifted a fluorescent green shell from its place by the door and pulled it on. The windbreaker would only give her a couple more weeks.

She pushed the door shut with her hip while she zipped up the front. She locked the door and dropped the key into the planter. Unoriginal, but better than having it bounce around in her pocket. The uneven sidewalk heaved up over tree roots. She doubted the city would ever get around to fixing them.

Sonya didn't much like running, but the fresh air felt good and it helped to keep her hips from mushrooming. The whole idea of becoming a paralegal had been driven by the desire to find a rich lawyer working his way up the corporate ladder. Find him, snag him, sleep with him, and marry him.

So far, she'd done her share of the first three, but the marrying bit seemed elusive. Then there were guys like Farwick. A bit old, but kind and obviously interested. The only problem was the wife. He already had one.

At least Farwick was decent enough to tell her up front. She wanted to let him buy her another drink. She felt like she owed him. Anyway, it sure was great to have someone who understood all that computer crap, so she didn't have to take it down to the computer hospital and pay some just-graduated punk more than she made in a week to fix the damn thing.

Sonya rounded the corner and passed the stone gardens of St. James before slowing down. A group of teenage boys hung around a bus stop, hitting hard on a girl who already had a kid in tow. The poor child was mostly forgotten.

Sonya waved to the girl, who looked vaguely familiar, which—considering her line of work—wasn't exactly a good thing. Chestnut was the short way home. Sonya had cramps and cramps needed ice cream, not running. Besides, Preston wanted router password.

Chapter 20

Ethel Maude Mallory managed to stave off interviews from local television stations paid off by the lottery officials to run a feel-good story. The reporter hadn't pressed that hard. After all, she only took home one hundred grand. It was amazing exactly how insignificant looking a pile of 1000, one hundred dollar bills could be.

Ethel Mallory had always imagined winning the lottery would finally put her mind at rest. Instead, she had to deal with reporters and suddenly friendly family members who vultured around after the news broke.

Ethel took the two bundles of cash and hid them under the shit covered paper in the parakeet cage.

Chapter 21

Jesús Santiago pulled into Solly's Mart at exactly five minutes past midnight. The fluorescent lights from the store spilled out to form large yellow squares on the sidewalk. Jesús parked in the handicapped spot directly in front of the double glass doors. A single padlock secured a chain wrapped through the crash bars on the inside. Solly's closed at midnight.

Jesús retrieved a paper gift bag from the passenger floor and stepped out. He scratched at a new tear tattoo under his right ear. Time to do some business. A ragged kerosene pump stood at the corner and Jesús rounded this and followed his nose to the dumpster area behind.

A shape resolved from the shadows and stepped toward him. "Did you bring what I asked for?"

"Maybe. You have the cash?" Jesús stepped a little closer.

"Stay there. Besides you don't really want to see me, do you?"

Jesús smiled. "Yes."

"Screw you." The voice didn't move. "The money is tucked under the dumpster. Sealed bag."

Jesús kept his eyes on the shadowy figure and toed around under the dumpster until he felt the bag. He kicked it into the open. "How am I supposed to count it in the dark?"

"You're not."

"And I'm supposed to trust you?" he asked.

"It's all there."

Jesús didn't bend over. The bag was by his feet. He had been listening to the voice. "How old are you?"

The voice didn't answer. Jesús waited. "I asked you a question."

"I'm younger than I sound."

Jesús shook his head. He needed the sale, but it was time to leave. He turned and walked quickly away, leaving the plastic bag next to the fetid dumpster. He had walked away before. Kid customers were like girls with AIDS. Better not to know them.

This kid was on his own.

Chapter 22

Preston Farwick flicked through the file directory of pictures. The girl loved her camera phone. All files had been dated and organized by month. "My, my, Sonya. Looks like you've had quite a few boyfriends."

His phone buzzed and Cookie, his shepherd, sat up, tongue lolling from the side of her mouth.

Farwick smiled when he saw the number. How fitting, he thought.

"Hey, there. Funny you called. I was just working on your computer. Looks like I might be able to save the picture files."

He listened. "Great, let me get a pen."

Farwick jotted the router's password down into the note book on his desk. "Perfect, got it. I'll probably be done sometime tomorrow. I can drop it off after work if you'd like. What time will you get home?"

He glanced at his calendar. "Good. Sounds like a date," he chuckled. "I'll see you then."

Chapter 23

Ashley only came on Saturday's.

A rusting wrought iron fence guarded the cemetery. She'd always wondered about it. Even before Lisa was buried here. Why would anyone want to put a fence around a cemetery? It wasn't like there was any danger of the tenants getting out.

Some of the stones in here dated back to the Civil War. She'd done a research paper on them in elementary school. Names like Eisenmengers, Simmons and Kutricks disappearing on crumbling tomb stones no one cared about anymore.

The letters on Lisa's marble stone stood crisp and clear and final. Someone donated it. Ashley bent down and brushed brown leaves out of the way. The grass looked perfect. They'd put four square pieces of sod in place over her sister's spot. Four square pieces. That was all it took to cover up Lisa's life.

The empty place for her sister pulled down on Ashley's stomach and made her feel empty. Wet grass soaked through her jeans, but she didn't care. She leaned back against the uncomfortable stone. Lisa seemed easier to remember here.

But try as she might, Ashley couldn't remember the sound of Lisa's voice in high school. Only early ones. Before mother got sick. Before any of it.

"Hi."

Ashley spun around. "Oh. Hi." It was Chase. Probably her best friend. Just one more person she'd treated like trash. One more burnt bridge.

He dropped his backpack beside her. She wasn't sure why he liked her. She could be mean and nasty to him and he always came back, acting like nothing had happened. That was until the last time. Since then, he'd stopped coming around.

"Sorry. I didn't know you'd be here," he said. Chase fished out a plastic grocery bag and untied the top. Mums. Purple ones. He picked off the buds that had broken on his way over. Red foil wrapped around the flower pot. His chapped fingers snuggled it up against Lisa's stone. "There you go," he muttered.

Chase shouldered the bag and walked away. Ashley tried to say something. She wanted to call him back, but nothing came out. Her own sadness and loneliness just swallowed up the sound.

The boy weaved through the graveyard toward the main gate.

"Chase!"

He turned and waited for her to catch up.

She ran to him.

"Thanks."

"Thanks for what?" he asked.

"The flowers."

"Oh." He shrugged. "They weren't for you."

"I know." Ashley blushed.

Chase stared, waiting for her to say something.

Ashley turned around, hunting for words in the graveyard. She rounded on him again, closed her eyes and pushed her hands deeper in her pockets. "I'm sorry I've been such a bitch."

Chase pulled off his glasses to wipe away imaginary smears.

"Will you— I mean, can you forgive me?" she asked.

Chase looked up at her again. He'd gotten a haircut and the top bits stood up around his crown. He seemed to be thinking. Then he nodded. "I already have."

"Then how come you haven't come by."

"Didn't figure you wanted me around after what I said. It was pretty stupid."

"No. You were right. What you said was true."

"True and kind aren't always the same thing."

She didn't respond. Kindness wasn't something she was doing especially well at lately. They walked toward the main gate.

"Ralph got inside," Chase said.

"He really hacked into the court computer system?"

"Yep. He started pulling data last Sunday night. He only works after the office closes. He doesn't want anyone else noticing him poking around."

"Where did you find this guy?" she asked.

"School."

"How did you talk him into helping?"

"Because he thinks you're hot, and—"A sheepish green spread over Chase's face, "I told him you were my girlfriend."

Chapter 24

Nick Rail and Pete Finnerty took the exit for Morris and pulled up to the stop light. The car had been a gift from Nick's parents. A 1967 muscle car with a red stripe running front to back, right up over the air scoop. Turning sixteen had been quite an event. A big party. Lots of girls. The car. Even a little alcohol. After all, his parents always said they'd rather he drink at home where they could keep an eye on him.

That's when he and Lana first hung out. Now they were steady.

"Dude. Crack the window. Smoke's burning my eyes," Nick complained.

Pete Finnerty rolled the window down to draw the smoke out. "We gonna head back to the garage and get some practice time in?"

"Not tonight. The folks have company of some kind. Don't want a lot of noise." The light turned green and Nick pulled out.

"Noise? We don't make noise. We make music."

"Wrong again. You are a drummer. You make noise. It's a nice rhythmic sort of thumping, but it is definitely noise. I make the music."

Pete sucked on his cigarette. "They have no appreciation for good sound."

"True, but they're old. What do you expect? At least they are nice enough to let us use the garage. All I have to do is wash Dad's car every Saturday. Not bad for rent, I figure."

Nick pulled in to Solly's Mart. Seth occasionally called to ask for a ride home. Seth was, after all, the band's lead guitar player and his cousin.

Seth saw them pull in and walked out of the mart. Across the street, the employees all wore matching shirts with the company logo stitched just above their name tags. Not at Solly's. Seth wore a black tee sporting a picture of his favorite heavy metal band. White faces. Long black hair. Not unlike Seth. In fact, the comparison was remarkable.

Seth climbed in the back and patted Nick on the shoulder. "I'm ready."

Chapter 25

Ethel Maude Mallory used to be a heavy sleeper. Her nightly routine included the normal old lady rituals and a shot of cheap liquor. But tonight she lay awake staring at the water stain on the ceiling of her bedroom. The roof on the trailer always leaked when rain came from the south east.

Lately, damp spots had been appearing on her sheets in the mornings. It would probably be better if she stopped drinking before bed. The old woman rolled over again, trying to avoid the smell of urine and her own sweat.

Ethel heaved herself into a sitting position and found the shot glass and liquor by the pinched light from the other mobile homes. Anxiety had settled into her chest. She poured another shot. Maybe it would do the trick.

She swallowed quickly and decided to use the bathroom one more time. The prospect of getting out of bed made her grumpy. Ethel reached for her cane and scooted toward the edge of the bed. She leaned hard on the cane, made a loud grunting noise and shuffled down the hall toward the potty room. Beth was out, again. The girl almost never slept at home. Seth was probably still working.

Ethel relieved herself and went to check on the bird cage one last time. The dining room was dark, but the outside door was open. Ethel stopped cold. A shadow bent over the bird cage, wrestling with the green twist ties she used to fasten on the bottom.

"You leave that alone," she went after it, unthinking, determined to save her money. The shadow startled and moved, exposing a face.

It came at her then. Ethel Maude Mallory lifted her arms to protect her face. The last sound she heard was the meaty thump on her head before she went down.

Chapter 26

"This is a little weird," Sonya Hernandez slipped into a seat near the back of the restaurant and far away from the too-loud juke box.

"Weird how?" Farwick took her coat and hung it on the booth hook. He sat down across from her.

"Well, nothing, aside from the fact that you're married, and I'm here with you. Other than that, it's fine."

The bitterness beneath her words didn't escape Farwick. "Hey, listen," he said. "This is just you paying off my services as a computer geek, right? I thought me buying you a drink was a pretty good deal."

"Deal, yes, but still weird."

"I guess you're not in the habit of dating married men?" He didn't wait for an answer. "Relax. This is nothing. I'm not trying to seduce you."

"Does your wife know you're here?" Sonya asked.

"Not exactly," Farwick reached across the table and ran his fingers over the back of her hand. "I'm sorry. This was a bad idea. I'll take you home." He stood and reached for his coat.

"Wait. I don't want you to leave yet. It's not like that. I mean I like you. I'm just the sucker who falls for married men."

"Let's keep this simple then," Farwick said. "Don't fall for me, and I'll do my best not to fall for you. We are here on business. Your computer being the pretense. We won't make a habit of it. I'll even try to pretend you're not beautiful."

Sonya's face brightened and she relaxed. "Sorry, just some bad experiences, that's all."

"No problem. I don't want to make you uncomfortable. Besides, I'm too old for you. We'll get drinks, and I'll take you home."

"Thank you, by the way," she said.

"For what?"

"For not lying to me about being married."

Preston smiled. "No problem. I'm the most honest cheater you'll ever meet."

Sonya laughed. It suddenly seemed much less complicated.

Chapter 27

The police arrived on the scene after an anonymous tip from a woman with a Spanish accent. She didn't identify herself. The trailer park usually didn't wake up this early on a Saturday morning and the presence of sirens and police cars seemed incongruous against the backdrop of mismatched mobile homes.

Ethel Maude Mallory won the lottery, alright. She'd apparently been bludgeoned to death with a broken table leg which had been left at the scene. Osteoporosis was not a friend of elderly victims. The woman's skull was crushed in multiple places. She lay in the living room, her once gray hair matted with blood. The rubber toes of her cane protruded from underneath like the foot of an aluminum robot who had the misfortune of being in the way when she fell.

The parakeet cage was open and empty. If there had been birds, they were gone now.

Outside a few trailer park residents nosed around in their pajamas, smoking cigarettes, looking for information and speculating. Obviously she'd been murdered for the cash.

The responding officer cordoned off the scene and called all the right people for a murder investigation. Wide yellow tape fluttered gaily in the morning breeze. *Police line, do not cross*. Officer Fred Miller from Morris Police Department spent a few minutes interviewing neighbors. Everyone knew who did it. Everyone knew about the money. Everyone knew Solly's Bastard. Apparently the kid even had the balls to report to work like nothing happened.

Miller called in a description for Seth Mallory. He turned over the scene to another officer who would wait for the county coroner and the district attorney. Nothing was to be moved until the coroner arrived and the crime scene people worked their magic. Miller was tired of this shit, and he wanted to get the punk who did it.

He climbed into the cruiser, called for back-up and sped off to Solly's Mart. Poor white trash or not, no one deserved to be killed like that. Back-up was right behind. Another cruiser blocked the mart's entrance. Their red and blue lights chased each other in circles around the convenience store.

Officer Miller marched to the front of the line at the counter with his badge out. "I'm looking for Seth." Not here for donuts today.

A slippery, overly-thin girl behind the counter shrugged and pointed out the back door. Officer Miller started running and radioed the others. He burst through the door and saw the boy running across the lot.

"Stop! Police!" He was going to tag the little bastard. Miller spent too much time in college playing football to let this long-haired weed boy get away. He was almost on him when Seth dropped into a ditch and scrambled into a drainage pipe that ran under the road.

"I didn't do it," the boy said.

"Sure you didn't." Miller got down on his knees and pulled out his flash light. Seth had crawled halfway through the corrugated pipe when another officer appeared at the far side. A flashlight beam cut into the gloom. Seth's legs were soaked with mud and filth from the foul seep. Miller pointed the light directly into Seth's eyes—a white face framed in stringy black hair. Black eye liner ringed blood shot eyes. His mouth opened, forming a silent appeal.

The boy screamed again, "I didn't do it!"

Chapter 28

Seth Mallory had tacitly admitted to being at the scene. The boy had motive. The kid even had a half bag of weed in his back pocket. Miller sent the kid downtown and returned to the store.

The line at the counter had disappeared. He returned to the anorexic at the register. "Call the manager." Adrenaline still pulsed through his system.

"He doesn't like to be called," she said.

"I bet he doesn't like to get closed down, either." Miller glared at the girl, who eventually sneered and reached for the phone.

Five minutes later, Solly Gamber showed up. He wore orange flip-flops and a stained flowered shirt over khaki shorts. He hadn't shaved and the man smelled like he could use a shower. Not exactly the tidy image one would want from a man involved in serving food. Or anything else for that matter.

"Mr. Gamber. I'm Officer Miller over from Trent. We have just arrested one of your employees in connection with the murder of Ethel Maud Mallory."

Gamber's face remained stony and unmoved. If he had an emotional connection to the boy, he didn't show it.

Miller went on. "Our notes indicate he left here last night with a couple of friends. We'd like to review your surveillance tapes for the last week."

"I don't have to give them to you."

"You are right. If you don't give those to me, I may be led to the conclusion that you have some part in this. I'm gonna see those tapes. It will either be because you gave them to me like a good citizen should, or because I got a warrant. A warrant might suggest I need to dig a little deeper into your business."

Chapter 29

Thomas Rail served as the regional Chief Operations Officer for the Texas Line and Refinery Consortium. The TLRC represented interests responsible for transporting oil, natural gas and bio fuels across 49 states, Hawaii being the only hold out.

The TLRC hired men with ambition to match the ever growing oil demand in a world where oil was gold and price was king. Thomas Rail was one of these. He thrived under the high performance outputs demanded by corporate and governmental greed. As such, he wasn't home when the police arrived.

A couple of officers reviewed surveillance tapes and managed to identify the two boys traveling with Seth Mallory. The boys left the mart together just an hour before the coroner's best estimate for the time of Ethel Mallory's death.

Officer's Miller and Markovic walked up to the house with pistols unsnapped. They didn't need a warrant because of the nature of the crime, but the judge had been willing, and they didn't want to have to deal with any legal maneuvering. The case should be a slam dunk, especially if they got a confession. This would be a big deal for the Morris Police Department.

The Rail family lived in a gated neighborhood where each plot had been artfully arranged to maximize privacy without missing the opportunity to display their wealth. Real copper spouting framed the curved brick walkways, exterior lighting, and stucco walls.

Sally Rail opened the door. A large Saluki growled unhappily behind her. The dog looked like a gray hound with feathered tail and ears.

"Mrs. Rail?" Miller asked. The woman was younger than he expected. Or maybe she had enough money to make herself look that way.

"Good morning, can I help you?"

"I'm afraid so. Mrs. Rail, we have a warrant for the arrest of your son as a person of interest in connection with the robbery and murder of Ethel Maude Mallory."

Chapter 30

Chase and Ralph walked through the garage and downstairs to the library. Darren was already waiting.

"Bad news," Chase said. "Nick called me this morning. His cousin got into trouble, and the police think he's involved."

"What kind of trouble?" Darren asked.

"His grandmother was killed. Murdered."

"Shit. What did Nick have to do with that?"

"Nothing; but he was with his cousin when it went down," Chase said.

"Damn." Darren stood up and paced the room. "Was it because of the game?"

"Yes. At least Nick thinks so."

"What's going to happen with Nick?"

"I don't know," Chase replied.

"I think this could work for us," Ralph said. "At least this is one record I don't have to go looking for. It gives us another circle."

Chapter 31

Officer Miller pulled into the ally beside two crumbling row homes. Jesús Santiago lived in a rented apartment hacked out from the main dwelling. Miller parked next to a purple, kid's bike complete with purple handlebar tassels.

The plywood porch sagged badly by the stairs. A grill backed up against the brick wall on the other end of the porch. Miller opened the screen door and knocked. A round elderly woman opened the door and eyed him suspiciously.

"Good morning. I'm Officer Miller." He tried a smile, but the woman's black eyes didn't comprehend his English or the smile. Not for the first time did Miller wish he remembered more from high school Spanish class.

Nothing. Miller tried again, "I'd like to see Jesús Santiago."

"Jesús?" The woman shuffled back from the door and pulled it open. She motioned with her head for him to come inside.

Miller followed the woman into her home. Rice steamed on the stove. Boxes and storage tubs idled in the room's corners. Plastic window film distorted the view through to the yard, but Miller could tell the grass hadn't been mowed all summer.

He wondered how many people called this home. The woman stood in the doorway to a living room and motioned with her head to a man sleeping on the couch. Then she walked back to the kitchen.

Miller moved to a ladder back chair on the opposing wall and sat down. Santiago wore nothing but his boxers and a tee shirt. Several backyard tattoos peeked out from under his sleeves and a silver chain held a crucifix with his namesake.

"Mr. Santiago?" Miller wanted to get on with this. "Jesús."

The man stirred and his eyes opened, staring directly at Miller.

"Qué demonios?" Jesús sat up and shouted a slurry of unhappy Spanish at the woman in the kitchen. She was probably his mother. "What are you doing here?"

"Nice to see you, too, Jesús."

"Listen, I didn't have anything to do with that kid."

"So you know why I'm here then?"

"It's all over the news."

"Well, the cameras at Solly's show you coming for a visit a few days before the murder."

"I was buying candy for my little girl."

"Right." Miller stared at the man's face. "Listen, why don't you ask your mom to make us some coffee. Maybe the caffeine will improve your memory. At this rate, it looks like I'm going to be here for a while. The store camera shows you park your car and head around to the rear of the store. I'm guessing that isn't where you find candy for little girls."

"Oh, man. I didn't do nothing."

"Jesús, we've had lots of conversations over the years. I really want to believe you. I know some of the stuff you're involved in, and I haven't busted you. But part of me wants to. Part of me wants to bust you real bad. Right now, all I need is a little cooperation. A little information. You give me that, and I might leave you alone for a while."

"Why should I help you?"

"You mean aside from the danger of being charged as an accessory to murder?"

"Listen, I didn't give the kid anything."

"Now we're getting somewhere. So you did meet the kid?"

"Yes. That's why you're here, right?"

"It is now. What kid are you talking about?" Miller asked.

"You know, that skinny white boy who wears the black stuff around his eyes."

"You recognized him, then?"

"Yeah, but I didn't let on. Kids like that are bad news."

"What did he want?" Miller took notes.

"Listen, Miller, I don't want to get involved in this."

"It's a bit late for that now, isn't it?"

Jesús looked outside, thinking. "The kid wanted to buy a gun."

"And you sold him one?"

"No. The kid had the money. All in a bag and ready to go."

"But you didn't sell him a gun?" Miller didn't take his eyes off the man.

"No. I already said that."

"Why not? You suddenly decide to start living right?"

Jesús grew agitated and got up to pace the small room. "I don't do business with kids."

Chapter 32

Thomas Rail made a few phone calls. Companies dealing in oil kept lawyers nearby. He had been referred to one Gerald Goll. The man flew in from Philadelphia for their first consult. He carried an eel-skin briefcase that matched his shoes.

Gerald's horn-rimmed glasses sat square on his clean shaven face. His short cropped hair was swept neatly to one side. He glanced at his watch as soon as Nick entered the room. The black letters across Nick's orange jump suit read, 'JUVENILE'. Nick sat uncomfortably with his hands cuffed to the chair behind him. The guard moved to stand at the doorway. He wasn't leaving.

Mr. Rail was all business. He determined to put as much distance between their son and Solly's bastard as possible. Thomas nodded to the attorney, "Let's get started."

"Here's the deal," Goll began the meeting without even acknowledging Nick's presence. "A robbery has been committed. Because a woman was killed in the course of the robbery, the case becomes a felony murder. It is based on an old law that's still on the books. Basically, if someone dies during the commission of another crime, you get a free upgrade. Felony cases are automatically tried in adult court. Adult court awards adult penalties. Felons are put away for a long time. Most likely life without parole."

Sally Rail stifled a sob and put a white hanky to her face. Thomas said nothing and watched as Gerald Goll opened his briefcase and pulled out a file. "The legal precedents for this type of case don't bode well. The only way to play this is for Nick to make a deposition pointing the finger at Solly Gamber as the only murderer."

"He *was* the murderer." Sally ruffled at the affront.

70

"Of course." Goll shot a glance at Thomas and looked back at his file.

"It appears this will be fairly straightforward. Once Nick is cleared of the murder, his case will be bumped back to juvenile court. Juvenile punishments are quite lenient. The alternative is not good."

Nick straightened in his chair. "I'm not going to throw Seth under the bus. His grandmother never gave him anything. She owed him that money."

Goll looked for the first time at his client. "Did you strike the woman?"

"Of course not," Nick scowled. "I'm not that kind of kid. I just happened to be there when it all went down."

"Will your finger prints be found on the murder weapon?"

"No. I wasn't even in the house."

"Where was Pete," Goll checked his notes before attempting the last name, "Finnerty?"

"I dropped him off before we stopped at Seth's place."

A sob interrupted the exchange. Sally's eyes were red from crying. "I still can't believe you would get involved in such a thing, Nick. I just can't believe you'd do that."

"Mom, I thought Seth was just going to ask his Grandmother for the money to go to music school. He didn't want to spend the rest of his life working at the mart."

The comment appeased his mother. The idea of it being an act of kindness helped to soften the sharp edge of the consequences her son was facing.

"Good." Goll moved the meeting back on point. "We'll arrange a formal deposition. I'll write up a statement for you to read. Chances are the prosecution will be happy to arrange a plea bargain in exchange for your testimony, and we can get your case sent back into juvenile court. They want to push this through and get a conviction. Your testimony will likely be key to their case."

"Then?" Thomas Rail wanted more.

"Then we'll be able to handle it. Depending on what the judge determines, Nick may get some community service or at most a couple of months in juvenile detention."

"A couple of months for a murder he didn't do?" Thomas raised his voice. "That's not acceptable."

"Mr. Rail," Goll turned his silvery stare on the boy's father, "your son drove Seth to the house and was present during a robbery and murder. Acceptable or not, those are your only options. If Nick cooperates with the deposition, the judge will likely take that into consideration."

Chapter 33

The Moderator printed off transcripts of his conversations with the player and put them in a manila folder marked, 'AMPED.'

Perfect. This was perfect. He would have to follow this one closely.

Maybe he could play this kid twice.

With Sonya Hernandez's computer working for him, that shouldn't be difficult. The Crime Records Department served as a clearing house for all the legal briefs, depositions, filings and such. If he wanted information on a case, Sonya's chair had the best view.

Most files were available to the public. But the Crime Records Department kept the lid tight on juvenile records. That suited him just fine.

Chapter 34

Nick followed Gerald Goll into the courtroom and sat down at the defendant's table. The bailiff called people to their feet and the judge entered.

She was a short, round woman in high heels. Nick thought her voice sounded a little raspy. Lana's mom wouldn't let her come to the adjudication hearing. They'd only been allowed infrequent phone calls in the ten days since the delinquency petition.

The judge read the charges against Nick Rail. It didn't sound good, but it could have been worse. The prosecution hadn't even bothered to bring murder charges.

Gerald Goll carefully painted the picture of a nice kid in the wrong place at the wrong time. Nick could feel the tension from his parents. They sat behind him in absolute silence, dressed well for the occasion. No need to give the impression of incompetent parents. In fact, Goll went to some lengths building a case for the strength of their family. Nick figured his family functioned reasonably well, but the embellishments got so thick Nick had to force back a smile.

Nick spent most of the hearing staring at the floor and willing himself to stay calm until it was over. Goll assured him juvenile hearings were simple, low risk affairs. Of course, that sounded good until the judge decided a detention facility would improve his sense of moral responsibility.

Judge Ramsey pulled off her bifocals and leaned over the bench to deliver her disposition. Nick stood.

"Nick, you seem like a nice boy. Remember, a man will always be judged by the company he keeps. Let this be a lesson to you. By order of this court, you will be required to complete 45 hours of community service. You will check in with a juvenile probation officer every month for the next year. At that point, we will evaluate your progress and determine if any further action is required."

Chapter 35

Snow came early to Pennsylvania. Fat, lazy snowflakes fell to mingle with the mess of leaves and muddy earth. After only an hour, white covered the ground and the world seemed to stop. Schools canceled classes, local officials pled with residents to stay off roads, clean-up crews got to work, and neighborhood kids gathered in noisy bundles to sled down any hill they could find.

No one came to visit Seth. No one wanted to speak on his behalf. Seth's mother hadn't shown her face, and he hadn't seen Nick, Pete or Lana since the murder.

Seth Mallory had long ago learned that no one listened to him, so he had decided to keep his mouth closed. When he opened his mouth in school, he just ended up in more trouble.

Seth's court appointed attorney led him in and out of meetings. Every meeting seemed important and every one had a label he didn't understand. Seth thought his attorney looked young and chic which he didn't figure was a good thing. Attorneys were supposed to be cold, hard and scary. Jennifer Post wasn't any of these. She wore a short grey skirt and matching jacket. Her compact was never far away, and she seemed more concerned with keeping him off death row than getting him out of jail.

He didn't speak to her either. Didn't answer questions. Didn't try to defend himself. His reluctance to speak irritated the judge.

He went numb and stayed silent through everything. Silence, Seth figured, was his safest option. Seth even listened to Nick's deposition with stony indifference.

The legal machinery worked its magic. It was an open and shut case: Seth's drugs, past incursions with the law, his case file as presented by a social worker Seth hadn't met, and Nick's deposition. According to witness testimony, Seth even tried to purchase a gun. Without a gun he'd used a table leg.

Every piece added a new angle to Seth's character. Each artfully presented by an attorney representing the Commonwealth, whoever that was.

After only three days of trial Seth was sentenced to life without parole.

Chapter 36

Seth Mallory somehow managed to wiggle away from the prison guards once they passed into the hallway. He bolted for the door. A red dot appeared near the small of his back just before the darts of the guard's taser tore through the orange suit. Tiny barbs lodged under his skin. Spun silver wire curled back toward the blunt gun. The guard pulled the trigger delivering 50,000 volts near Seth's spine. His body went rigid as the voltage scrambled his nerve signals. Incapacitated, Seth crumpled onto the floor. He lay there, waiting for the officers to pull him back to unwilling feet.

One guard stood on the chain between his legs while the other pressed a knee hard into the small of his back.

"You ready to come along now?" the guard asked.

Seth said nothing. Tears dripped off the edge of his nose and made a wet spot on the vinyl. He cried not for the pain, nor the insult of the stun gun. Ahead was the long empty tunnel of prison. The chains around his wrists felt heavy.

"Kid. You don't make the rules anymore. I ask you a question, you answer it. Right?"

No response. Seth's mind erupted in a flash as the guard pulled the trigger a second time. He could feel his body convulsing involuntarily. Could feel the warmth of his own urine spreading between his legs. The final shaming.

He could hear the guards talking behind him. "Looks like we have a non-compliant."

"Where's he going?" The other guard sounded older than the first.

"The Supermax."

"Already? He must have really pissed someone off."

"Yes. The judge. Kid wouldn't answer a single damn question. Judge made the recommendation himself."

The younger one addressed him again. "Okay, kid. I'm going to ask you one more time. You ready to come along now?"

Snot ran from Seth's nose down onto his lip. He nodded.

Chapter 37

The Moderator signed on to Sonya Hernandez's computer and then logged into the Crime Records Department secure database. For anyone in the court's IT department, it would look like Ms. Hernandez was there.

After a few minutes of browsing, he located the Seth Mallory and Nick Rail case files. He paused for a while to skim the court reports. Interesting.

Nothing anywhere about the money. No one seemed to know where it went.

"Thank you, Ms. Hernandez," he muttered. "It's been a pleasure doing business with you."

Chapter 38

Solitary confinement 23 hours a day. Seth Mallory stood in the center of his cell and turned, arms spread out. The restraints had been removed, but this was worse. A metal platform anchored to the wall held a plastic mattress. A folded grey wool blanket set squarely on the bunk's corner. The toilet in the corner already reeked. He hadn't even used it.

His door to the hallway had no knob on the inside. A single slide at the bottom facilitated the distribution of food. A tepid, oily soup in a paper cup rested on a flimsy paper tray. It sat there, untouched, getting colder.

He paced the dimensions with bare white feet on the hard floor. Almost 12 the long way. Nine the other. He wondered how many times he would pace it out.

Concrete walls echoed back the sound of naked feet.

Seth raised his left hand to an imaginary fret board and closed his eyes. Fingers settled into position. His right hand plucked the string.

Nothing.

Only silence. Cold, concrete silence.

Seth put two fingers up to his lips and sucked on an imaginary joint. It wasn't working.

Chapter 39

Ralph sucked powdered cheese off his finger and wiped his hand on his chest. An orange stain had grown across the shirt front as the bag of puffed cheesy curls emptied out.

"What are you finding?" Darren stared at Ralph's painted nails and decided he liked them.

"I've just created a mini program that will sift through the text of every file I find and sort the words by frequency."

"What's that for?" Darren asked.

Ralph chased the last chip around the bottom of the cheese bag and added to the shirt stain. "It will eventually create a conglomerate of common words like, counties, towns, organizations, etc. We can use this to make the search area smaller."

"Then what?"

Ralph stopped, distracted by his silhouette on the wall. He shook his head, watching the shadow-curls dance. He chuckled to himself. "I have no idea. Ask Chase."

Chapter 40

Nick Rail sat on the steps outside Lana's house. Her mother didn't want him inside. The air blew chill through his coat, and he shivered. Lana could talk for a few minutes but only a few. Her mom said they had to leave soon. No doubt to run some imaginary errand to keep her away from him.

The door opened again and Nick turned. Lana stood behind the screen.

"Hey," Lana said. An awkward smile.

"Can't you come out?" Nick asked.

Lana shrugged. Her eyes glanced sideways. Mom's listening. Watching.

They stood staring at each other—the screen door and too much other stuff between them. Her mother's fears, the scare of jail, the old lady's death, family pride.

Her lip quivered a little. Several times they moved to say something, then she mouthed the words, "I love you."

He nodded.

Lana held up crossed fingers, so he could see them, then they disappeared. She spoke loud enough for her mom to hear.

"Nick, I think it is probably best if we stop going out."

His nod was almost imperceptible. Then he brought his hands forward on an imaginary keyboard.

She nodded.

Nick turned to go, but she put her hand over her stomach and mouthed another message.

Nick squinted and turned his head to the side. Confused.

She mouthed the words again.

Nick's eyes got big. Comprehension. The words rang in his head as if she'd spoken them aloud.

I'm pregnant.

Chapter 41

Preston Farwick pulled into the farm lane. The owners of the empty property had been at a retirement home for years.

The countryside conspired to make this the perfect retreat. Situated down a lane and behind a woods, only the farm-house roof was visible from the road. This and the silo had fallen into disrepair, it now served as a home for pigeons and a trellis for an over-aggressive trumpet vine.

Farwick parked near the house. He grabbed a cardboard box and a canvas tool bag from the seat beside him. "Come on, Cookie." The dog bounded out of the silver minivan and tore across the yard, glad for space to run and play and sniff. She eventually settled enough to follow Farwick down through the field to a spring house sitting low in the meadow.

The spring house had been constructed from brown stone pulled from surrounding fields. A single tiny window lighted a kind of stone bench across the back wall for cold storage. Inside, the spring bubbled up into a square pool just beside the five foot door. Farwick pushed the door wide to add extra light.

He stood inside and examined the spring house. The solid pine door had a thin film of black mold growing up the inside. A few spongy patches of green moss clung to the stonework where a frail light passed across the wall. The twelve-inch window sat above the pool of cold, spring water.

The main house had pumped water from the spring instead of using a well. A black pipe snaked in from the outside just below the surface of the water. The water and the fact that three quarters of the house was underground kept the room at a steady 50 degrees even on the hottest of summer days.

Farwick set the cardboard box on the stone bench, pulled out the remote activated deadbolt and went to work.

Chapter 42

Lana retreated to the privacy of her room and locked the door. She had to see him. Opening her computer, she checked her social networking sites but realized he probably wouldn't use that anyway. Nick preferred privacy.

Then email. One from Nick from a new address.

Lana,

Got a new safe email in case parents are watching. Meet me behind Solly's Mart tonight at 7:30. Ignore everything else from 'me.'

I have to see you.

Nick

Chapter 43

Chase and Ralph stood leaning over the printer. The print tray filled with lists of words from the juvenile records Ralph located referencing some kind of computer game. He pulled Seth Mallory's file as a starting point and added seventeen others, including Ashley Blithe's. A light blinked orange and Ralph reached for an unopened ream of paper and tore off the wrapper.

"The list is about thirty-five pages long." Ralph beamed.

"I've heard the first twenty-five most common words make up twenty-five percent of all printed matter," Chase said, "and the first one hundred account for about half."

"Really?" Ashley seemed impressed.

Chase looked at the stack of paper as the laser printer kicked into gear. "Based on my research, we should be able to safely ignore the top three hundred words or so. After that we'll get a better aggregate of the data."

"Aggregate data?" Ashley piped up from her seat. "How did you fail English?"

"Commas," Chase replied without looking up from the printer. "And homework. I never did the homework."

"Let me guess, you were too busy reading up on early American storm drains or the life cycle of the inch worm." Ashley rolled her eyes.

"Physics, actually." The printer stopped and Chase grabbed the raft of paper from the tray. He set it down on the table and skimmed through the first few pages.

"What are you doing? I thought you said we could ignore the first half," Ashley chided.

"I am, mostly."

"Mostly?"

"Rule number one is never trust statistics. What we *can* do is ignore all the unique words." He separated off the last seven pages that had no match and stapled them together. "Great. I'm taking this with me. Email me the file as well, okay, Ralph?"

"For you? Not a chance." Ralph replied. He looked over at Ashley and whistled as his finger followed her figure to the floor. "For your girl? Anything at all."

Ashley had been kind enough to play along with their little ruse about being Chase's girlfriend, but he could feel the blush rising under his ears.

Ashley gave Ralph her best bored stare. "Ralphie, you need lessons in how to get a girl."

So do I, Chase thought. So do I.

Chapter 44

Lana convinced her mom she was heading to the mall and got a friend to drop her off near Solly's. Thankfully her mom had relaxed a bit since her conversation with Nick that afternoon. She'd wanted them to break up ever since she heard about the incident with Seth's grandmother.

Lana buttoned her jacket and hurried around to the back of the store. A black man with shoulder length dreadlocks worked a broom around the dumpster.

He glanced up over the top of his sunglasses. They must be for show. It was already dark.

"Can I help you?" The man seemed friendly enough.

"No thanks." Lana stopped. "Actually, maybe you can. I'm supposed to meet someone around here."

"You got a name?" The janitor spoke again.

"Yes. Why?" She was suspicious. Don't talk to strangers, right?

"Because I've got a message, but it's only for someone with a certain name." He pulled a folded paper from his pocket and rechecked the name.

"I'm Lana." She took a step toward him.

"Lana what?"

"Lana Summers."

"Well, Lana Summers, a certain Nick asked me to give you a ride to where he's waiting. Said something about not wanting your mom to see you getting into a car with him. All sounded kind of strange to me, but I told him I would."

Lana hesitated. "I thought he was going to meet me here."

"Like I said, it sounded strange to me. I told this Nick I wouldn't want no daughter of mine climbing into a car with some stranger. No sir." He went back to sweeping. "That boy's probably trouble anyway. You should just go on home, child."

"No. It's not like that. He's really a nice guy."

"Still, if your mama found out you climbed into a car with a black man, she gonna freak."

"Please, would you take me?"

#

Lana Summers followed the man to an adjacent lot. "The boss don't like us taking up the customer's parking," he explained.

She climbed in and buckled up. The thought of seeing Nick again made her smile.

"Thanks for taking me," she said.

"I don't much like helping kids sneak behind their parents' backs. I just hope you guys aren't doing anything illegal," the man said. "I don't want no parts of that."

"Of course not. It's just my mom isn't real happy with Nick right now."

"If you say so." The man began to hum a little tune as he headed out of town.

"Where is he?" she asked.

"Just about fifteen minutes from here. Maybe less. I must be some kind of crazy doing this for ya'll."

Lana gave the man her best smile. He had a kind face, at least what part of it she could see in the dark. He pushed his sun glasses down on his nose so he could drive.

"You have any children?" she asked.

He shook his head. "If I had children of my own, I'd probably have enough sense to not get mixed up in this kind of funny business." A hint of a smile. The man relaxed a little. He looked at her, studying her face. "But I guess you seem okay."

"What is your name?" Lana asked.

"My name? Why? So you can tell your mama?" The grin again.

"Something like that."

"It's something," he replied. They turned off the road and down a bumpy lane. Obviously the man didn't want to give his name and Lana decided not to press him. She strained her eyes in the dark for Nick.

"Where is he?" she asked.

"He said he was going to meet you in the spring house."

"What's a spring house?"

"That's a little shack people threw up over a spring to keep the water clean. They used it for milk before there was such a thing as refrigeration."

"I see," she replied, though she didn't really get it.

The man parked the van and turned it off. "That's it down there." He pointed through the window into the dark.

"I can't see anything."

"Well, I suppose you probably want me to walk you down there, too." He sighed and opened the door. "Come on, then."

He led the way down a rough path. The moon slept somewhere out of sight. Lana followed close behind, growing more excited to see Nick.

"I don't know if he's here yet, but this is the place." He stopped in front of the spring house.

"It's pretty dark." Lana felt the quiet of the fields and woods around them without really seeing any of it.

"Why don't you check inside? Maybe he's here already." The man pushed open the springhouse door.

Lana peered inside. "Nick?" She spoke his name into the black.

Lana felt her arm being twisted hard behind her. Fingers pulled the phone from her back pocket. The grip tightened, he pulled her arm up hard and pain slashed through her shoulder. Lana screamed. She tried to twist away, but he grabbed the back of her jacket and shoved her in. The door frame smashed against her head on the way through. Sparks swirled, competing with the darkness and the pounding pain. She heard the metal on stone of the door's bolt sliding into its place, effectively locking out the entire world.

"What are you doing?" she shouted, scrambling backward on all fours until she crashed into something hard. "Leave me alone. Don't touch me." Breathless words.

Her wide eyes cast about in the darkness, waiting for him to come at her again. She kicked wildly, with her back on the ground. She screamed, "Get away from me."

"My pleasure." The muted voice sounded far away.

It took her a full two minutes to realize the man hadn't followed her inside.

Chapter 45

Lori Summers waited until 1:30.

She needed her ex-husband now, and she hated it. At 1:31 she dialed his number.

Lori spoke as soon as she heard the phone make connection. "Ron, where's Lana?"

"Excuse me?" It was his wife. "Do you know what time it is?"

"Of course, I'm sorry. It's just Lana didn't come home tonight." She waited for the words to register. The phone muffled a distant conversation.

"What's going on." It was Ron. No greeting. Fact-based conversation.

"Lana didn't come home tonight. She said she was going to a mall with Katie, but never came home."

"Why didn't you call Katie?"

"Sarcasm. You're really going to use sarcasm on me at a time like this? Of course, I called her."

"And?"

"She didn't know anything about the mall. Lana asked Katie to drop her off somewhere over in Morris."

"In Morris? What the hell would she be doing over there?"

"I have no idea."

"This isn't about that boy, is it?" Ron knew about Nick.

"I don't think so. I overheard them breaking up today. Besides, he lives in Trent."

"Call the police. I'll be over in 25 minutes."

Lori hung up. Her breathing came in shallow gasps. This can't be happening, she thought. She had to call the police, but she wanted to run out the door and scream Lana's name.

She dialed 911.

Chapter 46

Lana Summer studied the sky through the spring house window. The orange glow of light pollution reflected off the canopy of clouds. No light came inside. A dank, earthy smell filled the room as completely as the darkness.

Her hand studied her throbbing forehead. Sticky something. She dipped her finger in her mouth and tasted it. Blood.

Damp, cold air pressed in around her and she shivered. She stuffed stiff fingers in her armpits. I need to stay warm, she thought.

Was the man going to come back? She didn't want to think about it. Couldn't. Maybe she could climb to the window. She pushed away from the rock wall and walked toward it.

She took another step. Darkness swirled. Nothing made sense. A sighted girl in a blind world. The ground opened up in front of her and she fell. Icy water enveloped her and something scratched a deep angry welt on her side.

Wild panic engulfed her. Lana fought, kicking and clawing against frigid water that turned her clothes into dead weight and her muscles into lead. She gagged, choked and scrabbled her way to the pool's edge. Slippery rocks and icy sharp fingers fought against her. Fingernails dug into the dirt floor beyond the pool, clawing and pulling against the cold-wet that sucked breath from her lungs. She heaved herself over the edge and lay panting, listening to the sound of water dripping from her and the sound of screaming in her head. A fingernail had been torn almost off and flopped hopelessly near its base. She touched it and sent stinging fire up her finger.

Hot vomit filled Lana's throat. Burning and wretched, it pressed up to spill over her arms and into the dirt. Again her stomach cramped, throwing up more fear and water and panic.

Chapter 47

Lori and Ron Summers sat on opposite sides of her kitchen table while Officer Sinclair filled out the necessary paperwork. Name, age, description, clothing worn on the date last seen.

It all sounded too final.

"We're wasting time here," Lori folded her arms. "I don't know exactly what she was wearing when they left."

"And why is that, ma'am?"

"Because I was in the shower."

"So it is possible that the child didn't actually leave with Katie Johnson."

"No. Well, I suppose so, but Lana doesn't lie to me. She's not like those kids who run away from home."

Officer Sinclair glanced at his laptop and made another note.

"Why can't we just get out there and start searching?" she asked.

"I have already called it in. We already have police working that area."

"Why aren't you out there looking? We have no idea what could be happening to her right now." Lori shot an angry look at Ron. Get involved, she thought. Say something. He didn't or wouldn't take the hint. Dead beat piece of –

"I'm well aware of the dangers, Mrs. Summers. Federal law mandates we immediately complete a missing person report to file with the NCIC."

"That's 'Miss,'" Lori corrected. "We're not married."

"What's the NCIC?" Ron actually talked.

"The National Crime Information Center. It's a centralized database that all law enforcement agencies have access to. If Lana has been abducted, this is the best way to get this information out to the most people."

"What about that Nick Rail kid?" Ron asked.

"I'll have an officer stop by to check that lead. But you've told me the Lana and Nick are no longer dating. Is that correct?"

"Yes, I heard them break up yesterday." Lori replied. "They both seemed pretty calm about it."

"Does Lana have access to a computer here?" Sinclair asked.

"Yes. She has a laptop for homework."

"Would you mind if I take a look?"

"It's in her room."

"Does she use a password?" The officer asked.

"Yes, I think so."

"Do you have this password?"

Silence.

Ron exploded. "You have got to be kidding me."

The officer intervened. "Well, it won't do me much good, but if you can get it for me, I'll take it to the station. I'll have to track down someone to take a look at it. We don't have a cyber-detective on our team, but Florin has one we can outsource to."

Lori went back to Lana's room. The empty room. An officer and her ex-husband in the kitchen. Lana gone. It all seemed surreal. At any moment, Lana could appear at the front door. Or..." She pushed the thought back, unplugged the power cord and scooped up the laptop. "Where are you?" she whispered.

Then the tears came.

Chapter 48

Preston Farwick took Lana's phone into his office and deactivated the GPS. Then he turned off his portable jammer that had covered her signal until then. The jammer was about the size of a walkie talkie and, though it had a limited range, it was perfect for what he needed.

He looked over at Cookie. "You can get anything on the internet these days," he said.

The brown spots over the German shepherd's eyes moved up at the sound of his voice, but she didn't lift her head.

Farwick gutted the girl's phone data and saved it to his desktop. He might need these numbers.

He poured himself a shot of ten year old Irish whiskey, and settled into the couch.

Cookie shuffled over and sat next to him. She lifted one paw and put it on his arm.

Farwick scratched around the dog's ears. "Now leave me alone, Cookie. I need to get some sleep."

He would normally have gone to bed, but if he figured it right, his phone would ring soon.

Chapter 49

Officer Ken Dixon read the missing person brief as soon as he came on shift. Some of the officers had become a little callus to the Amber alert. Especially if the kids were older. The constant stream of delinquents running away from home so they could do what they wanted wasted huge amounts of time and money and kept police from their real work.

But every now and then, a report came through that had a different ring. If the kid wasn't in foster care and didn't have a previous record; if she had decent report cards and was involved in school; if the kid was a girl. Enough of the 'right' dots, and his buddies would drop everything to find her.

Dixon hated to admit that's how it worked, but it was the age old 'cry-wolf' thing.

This one had the right dots. At least in Dixon's mind. While Lana wasn't exactly a stellar kid, she probably wasn't the type to just skip out and not come home one night.

His phone beeped and Sinclair's name flashed on the screen. Sinclair was the officer from Trent who filed the report.

"Hey, Sinclair."

"Dixon. You saw the alert for Lana Summers?"

"Yes, I got it. What's your feel on this?"

"I think we've got a live one."

"Right. That's what I thought. What do you need?"

"I need your computer guy to look at her laptop. It's password locked. You think Chief Gregson will mind?"

"No problem. He'll probably want to cross-bill your department, but that's just because he does things by the book. But he won't mind. This kind of shit really pisses him off."

"Great. If you wouldn't mind waking your guy, I'll bring the computer over within the hour."

"Done."

Chapter 50

Preston Farwick woke to his burbling phone. Both hands on the analog clock hovered over the number two. "Right on time." He wished it had taken them just a little longer and he let a few rings pass before he picked up. "Farwick here."

He listened, grunting here and there.

"You sure this kid isn't just hanging out with friends or something?" he asked. A smile touched Farwick's eyes.

"Okay," he sighed. "I'm on my way."

Farwick hung up the phone, stretched and pulled on shoes.

He sat down to his own desk before heading to the office and opened the link to remote surveillance. He had mounted a simple pen cap-sized infrared camera inside the spring house. The wide angle lens made the room look round, but there was no place for her to hide.

He waited for the link to establish and studied the image. The girl sat curled up on the corner of the stone ledge.

"Sleep tight, little girl. Don't let the bed bugs bite."

Farwick turned to his dog. "Time to go to work, Cookie. Wanna come?"

Cookie didn't move.

Chapter 51

Officer Sinclair left Lana's anxious parents to visit the Rail home himself. He determined to stay focused on following the best leads. Others were out driving the streets. It was his job to turn up something helpful.

Sinclair turned down into the ritzy residential area of Trent. Most of the houses had fancy exterior lighting, definitely not the cheap solar lamps he planted next to his walkway.

He pulled into the Rail's drive and parked by the first bay of the three car garage.

"Time to wake up the neighbors," he said.

Concrete planters with spiraling topiary flanked the door. White lights blinked from behind the foliage.

Sinclair pressed the doorbell.

He could hear it ring inside, like church bells, only kinder. A dog barked and a porch light came on.

Eventually the door opened. Sally Rail stood wrapped in a silk house coat behind the screen door. She paled noticeably when she saw the officer.

"Can I help you?" she asked. A saluki stood at her heel.

"Yes. Sorry to disturb you. I'm following up on a missing person report for one Lana Summers. I'm aware that she and your son were friends."

"Lana Summers is missing?"

"Yes, ma'am."

"Oh God, since when?"

"Yesterday. Could I talk to Nick? They were friends, right? Maybe he might know something."

"He's sleeping."

"I'm sure you won't mind waking him for me, considering the circumstances." Mrs. Rail hesitated before showing Sinclair into the parlor. "Mr. Rail is out of town on business," she said by way of explanation. "I'll go wake Nick."

She left Sinclair and disappeared into the rambling house.

Nick came in wearing plaid flannel loungewear and a tee shirt.

"Hi, Nick. I'm Officer Sinclair."

"Hey. What's going on? Mom said something happened to Lana." He eyed the police officer warily.

"Yes. Lana's missing. She told her mom she was going to the mall last night, but she got dropped off somewhere in Morris."

"What? Why would she go to Morris?"

"I was hoping you could tell me that. Does she have friends in Morris?"

"No. I mean, not anymore."

"Not anymore?" Sinclair prodded.

"Well, one of our friends got into trouble and ended up in jail. He used to live in Morris. He was my cousin."

"Would she have gone to visit his family?" Sinclair asked.

"He doesn't have any. Not really. They're a waste."

"Lana's mother said you guys broke up yesterday. That so?"

Nick looked at his finger nail before answering. "Not exactly. We were just trying to keep her mother happy. She didn't want us together anymore."

"How did you usually communicate with Lana?"

"Social sites. Phone. Text. Mostly we just talked. I asked her to email me before I left yesterday." He buried his hands in his hair.

"I see, and have you heard from her?"

"No. I checked just before I went to bed."

"What time was that?"

"I don't know. One, maybe." Nick got up and paced the living room.

"Any idea why she didn't contact you?"

"No." His face fell.

"Where were you last evening?" Sinclair asked.

"What are you saying, officer?" Mrs. Rail broke in. "I don't appreciate the insinuation."

"Ma'am. If it were your daughter, you'd want me to find out as much as I could. It's a fair question."

"He was at home," Mrs. Rail snapped. The saluki growled.

"Were you here as well?" Sinclair probed.

She stopped, affronted, and hesitated before answering, "I was at the salon, but Nick stayed home."

"Okay, thank you. Nick, do you have any idea where Lana might have gone?"

The boy palmed his forehead, fear starting to take hold. "Did you call Pete Finnerty?" Nick asked. "He lives over near Morris, but it's in the Trent school district."

"She friendly with him?" Sinclair asked.

"Yeah, I guess. Pete was the drummer in our band." An angry shadow crossed Nick's face, but he forced it back with a plastic smile.

"Why don't you give me his address?" Sinclair held out a notepad and pen.

Nick wrote it down.

"You want me to call him?"

"Sure. Go ahead," Sinclair replied.

Nick pulled out his cell and dialed the number.

No answer.

Sinclair stood and handed Nick his card. "Thanks for your time. If you hear of anything, please give me a call."

"Is there anything I can do? I'm going to go crazy just sitting here." The boy was desperate. Worried. He didn't know anything.

A good sign. And not. Now Sinclair was back to square one.

"You can wrack your brain and call me if you think of any place she might have gone."

Nick nodded. Sinclair paused and put his hand on the young man's shoulder. "I'm sorry. We'll keep looking."

Sinclair nodded to Mrs. Rail. "I'll see myself out."

Chapter 52

Lori and Ron drove separately. They could cover more ground that way, and they didn't have to do it together.

Lori Summers turned onto the main street running through Morris. The street served as a thoroughfare for trucks moving from several local distribution centers to the main east-west artery for the state. At this hour trucks owned the road. The thought that her daughter could have been carried off in any of the sleeper trucks and might now be in another state screamed inside her head. She resisted the urge to chase down every truck and demand to look inside.

Stick to the plan, she told herself. Lana was probably okay. Lana had just done something stupid. Katie didn't know what Lana was up to, but it was, after all, Lana's idea to stop in Morris. She probably hadn't been abducted.

She alternately prayed for Lana and raged against her. Long, elegant, in-your-face lectures. Lori couldn't decide. Fear or anger. Anger and fear. In the end, she settled on both.

Lori glided through a red light without seeing it. Blazing white headlights slipped across her face and a truck horn blared. Lori came back to the moment.

Find Lana.

Just find Lana.

Chapter 53

"Pete, I want to talk to Lana." Nick decided on the direct approach.

"What the hell are you talking about?" Sleep grogged Pete Finnerty's voice.

"Lana." He said the name clearly. "Put her on the phone."

"Are you high or something? You've got the wrong number."

Nick's anger melted into something like panic. "She's gone missing. I thought she was with you."

"Why would she come here, you wack job?"

"The police will be there in a minute."

"What? Why?"

"Because she's gone missing. She didn't come home last night." Nick choked on a sob. "We don't know what's happened."

"Holy shit." Pete's voice woke up, "Holy shit."

Nick ended the call.

Now what?

Chapter 54

Preston Farwick arrived at the office around three a.m. Normally he didn't work these hours. Most computer questions could wait. Dixon left him a text saying the girl's computer was in Farwick's office.

Time enough for coffee, he thought. After all, what was the hurry? He jammed a white filter into the pot and inhaled the smell of the dark roast. The girl wasn't going anywhere.

Lana Summer's laptop sat on his office chair, avoiding an over cluttered desk. He already knew what was in there. At least some of it.

Farwick shoved several folders to the side, clearing a workspace. Then he opened the lid and plugged the computer into a desktop power strip. He returned to the kitchenette and found a mug from the eclectic collection in the cupboard. Someone bought it for the Chief and he'd re-gifted it to the coffee commons. Bold red letters on white declared: *'Me Boss, you not.'*

"Time to work some magic." He returned to his desk and pushed the start button on Lana's computer. Pressing F8 bypassed the usual start-up to run in safe mode. Then he clicked START and RUN and typed 'control userpasswords2.'

Almost everything he did could be found online, but knowledge was power and he wasn't about to give it away. Not now. Not when he was this close.

A simple document labeled 'pass' rested on the top right of the desktop display. It had passwords to everything. "I'm amazing," he said aloud. Farwick paused to sip his coffee, enjoying the thrill of being inside someone else's world. The green progress bar grew as he copied everything onto a slim, portable hard drive. He would sift through the rest of it later when there wasn't the chance that someone might walk in on him.

Farwick opened her email account and printed off the last email he had created from 'Nick.'

This was going to be interesting. Even Nick's lawyer was going to have trouble talking his way out of this one.

He paper-clipped a note to the email and dropped it on Dixon's desk. Then he had second thoughts. He pulled the sticky note with the name and number of the officer who filed the report. "I had better call this in," he said aloud. "Wouldn't want something horrible to happen to that little white girl, would we?"

He freshened up his coffee and picked up a magazine. The office was empty. It wouldn't hurt for the rest of them to imagine it had taken him a little longer to hack the computer.

Those Columbians make some damn fine coffee, he thought. He lifted his feet, put them on the desk, and opened the magazine.

Chapter 55

Seth Mallory settled onto the floor of the cell, aware of a new clarity of mind. The long hours of solitary had brought a keen focus. The trailer park, the job, the drugs, and his mess of a family seemed like another life. The profound solitude was like the death of a loved one. Suddenly everything in the world looked different. Clearer.

He closed his eyes, put his lips together, and blew out. A single low note, long and clear and warm hung in the air about him.

Seth clapped his hands together in self-congratulation like a little kid. Then he got up and his body began to move in a victory dance, slow and deliberate. His first whistle.

He'd never really danced before. Never in celebration.

Now he had something. Music they couldn't take away.

Chapter 56

Lana Summers startled awake with a jolt. Cold, like iron bands, wrapped itself around her. A film of light replaced the inky dark and she could make out the edges of her confinement. The window, she saw now, was too small to climb through. The spring-fed cistern no larger than a kiddie pool.

A shiver shook her body at the memory of falling in. She lifted her shirt and studied the bruised purple smear around the welt. The light grew incrementally until she could see the bit of plastic pipe that had been responsible for the welt. Lana found herself relieved that it hadn't been a creature of some kind.

She forced herself to stand and get the blood flowing. She found it then. A blanket on the other end of the shelf.

It didn't matter if it came from the pervert that locked her in here. She fumbled herself into it and remembered the last time she and Nick had snuggled together.

Nick. She had come here to see Nick. Maybe the creep was going to kidnap him as well. Vaguely she hoped he would. She desperately wanted to see Nick. Wanted to get out of this place. Maybe Nick had been attacked. Killed.

"God help me," she whispered. Her mind wandered to the man with the Rastafarian hairdo and the funny crocheted hat.

The shivering didn't stop. She needed to take off her wet clothes to get warm. Not going to happen, she thought. Any minute that creep could come back. She didn't want to give him a head start on whatever he might have in mind. The thought made her feel sick again.

Chapter 57

A wet, grey dawn broke slowly through the sullen clouds with no promise of sunshine. Officer Sinclair dropped the phone into his pocket and cursed his naiveté. Florin's cyber guy worked fast. He'd found an email from Nick. The kid knew something. Sinclair called dispatch and asked them to send an officer over to watch the house while he went through the proper channels to get an arrest warrant. The judge wouldn't flinch. Sinclair had pulled Nick's record. The kid wasn't as clean as he seemed.

Sinclair spun the wheel, aborting his land search for Lana and headed back to the office. He'd pick up a copy of the email from his fax machine and complete the warrant paperwork at the station. His shift was almost over, but he didn't care. He personally wanted to pick up the kid and watch him try to lie his way out of this one.

Sinclair pulled into his parking spot. He went straight into his office, shut the door and dialed the number for Lana's mother. She was probably going out of her mind.

She picked up after the first ring. "Did you find her?"

"No, Ms. Summers, I'm afraid not. But we have found an email on her computer that indicates she was trying to see Nick."

"That's ridiculous. I heard them break up myself."

"What time was that?" he asked.

"Yesterday afternoon."

Sinclair picked up the faxed copy of the email. "This was written yesterday at 5:30." He read it to her.

"I'm going to kill him," she said.

"That's probably not a great idea," he replied. "He just might be the only person who actually knows where she is."

"Who exactly initiated the breakup?" Sinclair asked.

"She did. Do you think he was angry and . . ."

"Not sure. Just hunting for a possible motive. We're going to pick up Nick this morning and keep him handy for a while. I'll keep you posted."

"What can I do?" she asked, desperate.

"You can get some sleep."

"Officer Sinclair," her voice iced over, "you don't have a daughter, do you?"

The phone clicked off.

Sinclair stared at the three girls smiling back at him from gold picture frames. He rubbed his eyes and dialed the number for the judge.

Chapter 58

Ashley ran most of the way to Chase's apartment. Finicky, his Jack Russell, barked non-stop inside, clearly unaccustomed to early visitors. She heard Chase scold the dog out of the way and then the door opened. Chase wore only a towel. Water dripped from his hair and down onto his chest.

"Oh," Chase said. He gripped the towel at his waist. "Why aren't you on your way to school?"

Ashley stepped out of the common hallway and pushed the door shut. Chase's eyes got big.

"Chase. Nick's girlfriend has gone missing. Nick called Darren who called me. Do you think it's *him*?"

"Who?" Chase fumbled for his glasses with a free hand.

"The Moderator." She glanced down at his towel. "You can't come like that. Get dressed; we're meeting at Darren's house."

"What about school?" he asked.

"Screw it. This is more important."

Finicky grabbed the towel's edge and pulled. Chase shoed him away. "Not funny, Finicky. Not funny."

Chapter 59

"I've never seen this before in my life." Nick held a copy of the email attached to the warrant. Even to him his words sounded fake. Forced. His mind felt foggy. This was too much. "Where did you get this?"

"From Lana's computer. I'll need you to come with me." Sinclair was tired.

"Wait a minute. How do you know this is from me?"

Sinclair sighed. "It has your name on it. Who else would send it?"

"I don't know. Some crazy guy who wants to get his hands on Lana. What makes you think I'd want to kidnap her?"

"You admitted that you didn't want to break up. I have no way of knowing if that was Lana's sentiment."

"How could I have kidnapped her if I'm here right now?" Nick's face got red. They were going to put him in jail and he'd already had enough of that. As long as they had him, they wouldn't be looking for whoever had Lana.

Sinclair didn't answer the question. "Listen, I'm willing to take you without handcuffs, if you're willing to cooperate."

Nick took a breath and fought for control. "Fine. At least let me get some proper clothes on."

Sinclair nodded. A humorless smile. "I won't leave without you."

Nick retreated down the hall, leaving his mother sniffling on the couch while trying to reach his dad somewhere in Texas.

He went into his room, closed the door and tried to think. He couldn't help Lana if he was sitting on his ass in jail. He pulled his phone, an email blinked in his inbox. The timing was uncanny. The sender's address was made up of bizarre characters and number sequences.

Nick tensed. He lost focus on everything else while he read it again. The email contained a single line. *Looking for Lana?*

Nick glanced at the time stamp and hit reply. *Who the hell are you?* he wrote. Maybe the guy was still online. Whoever it was had Lana.

The room swirled around him.

Nick looked at himself in the mirror and made a decision. He would run. The image disappeared as he yanked the door aside and threw a backpack on his bed. Wallet. hat. Jacket. He grabbed a money bank in the shape of a football from his bookshelf. Frantic fingers prized the plug and tore out the money, stuffing it loose into the pack. What else? His eyes shot around the room and came to rest on a short-handled battle axe, fashioned after the best the Middle Ages had to offer. It was a relic of sorts, and looked cool on the wall. But it was real.

Time to make it work, he thought.

A knock at the door. "You've got three minutes." The officer was in a hurry.

"I'll be right out. Feeling kind of sick to my stomach." He glanced toward his bathroom door, pushed the button and pulled it closed, locked. He shouldered his pack, picked up the axe and crawled through his bedroom window.

A birch tree—leaves bare for the winter—leaned close enough to reach. The smaller branches scratched at his face, and he dropped the last ten

121

feet to the grass. Ducking low, he circled the garage and hid behind the police car. Thank God, he thought. The cop hadn't parked him in. He gripped the axe handle and swung the blade at the cruiser's tire. It bounced off the hard rubber.

"Damn it," he whispered. Now using the edge of the pointed blade, he shoved the axe toward the tire. A satisfying hiss of air answered his efforts. No time to watch it deflate.

He scrambled through the garage's side entrance, climbed into his car and pushed the button on the visor for the garage door. The game was on. A strange exhilaration rushed over him. He would make it out, find Lana, and then apologize for running away.

It was his only chance.

The muscle car growled to life, sending an explosion of black smoke. Tires squealed on the concrete floor, and he barely cleared the retreating garage door. He watched his rearview mirror as he drove. Nothing. With any luck the officer would be waiting at the locked door of his bedroom, or banging on the bathroom door. It would take him a few minutes to get outside. The car screeched into a slide when he turned onto the road.

Nick cleared the neighborhood and slowed down. No sense drawing attention to himself. He made several turns to make sure he wasn't being followed. In only a few minutes, the whole world would be after him. For the first time, he cursed his car. Not exactly the type to blend in.

He headed for the highway and went West, taking a bridge that spanned the Susquehanna River. He pulled his phone and gave it a toss. It spiraled over the concrete guard rail down into the brown water. With any luck, the water proof case would keep it dry and floating with its signal leading police in the wrong direction.

Chapter 60

Chase set copies of Ralph's word list on the study table and spread another on the floor. "You sure you're parents aren't going to show up?" Ashley said.

"Positive. They don't believe in sick days."

"I do," Ralph said. "I only hope the school buys my story about small pox."

"Small pox?" Ashley scowled. "Why small pox? The biohazard teams are probably raiding your house as we speak."

"It was the first thing that came to mind. What did you tell your parents?" Ralph asked.

"Nothing." Ashley avoided the question. She didn't want to admit that her parents let her stay home when she wanted. God knows there'd been days after Lisa died Ashley just didn't want to get out of bed at all. They seemed to get it. Funny, she thought, for the first time, her parents actually seemed to trust her. Being trusted, she had to admit, was the last thing she expected.

"What are we looking for?" Darren still wore a pair of baggy sweats.

"Patterns," Chase replied.

"What kind of patterns?" Ashley asked.

"Names, mostly. I think those are our best bet. Ralph's program can't separate proper nouns, but you can skim the words until you find a capital letter."

Darren shuffled through the lists. "There's a whole bunch of names repeated more than once."

"Most of those are names of the kids in the file and their family members," Chase said. "We're looking for names of people indirectly connected to the case. Schools, or places, or organizations that might have something to do with all of them."

Chase hovered over his own copy of the list and started making notes on a poster paper he'd taped to the coffee table.

Chapter 61

Nick parked in the employee parking lot behind the mall and worked up a story to tell if someone challenged him. A sales clerk leaned against a yellow truck barrier smoking a cigarette. The clerk ignored him. Break time. Nick walked past him into the mall's service and delivery entrance.

Thankfully, no one did. He needed to email his dad for help. He slipped into a pharmacy and paid the cashier the five dollars for a half hour of time on the store's Internet. He opened a browser. Seth Mallory had introduced him to TOR. The Onion Router. Easy invisibility.

He accessed a secure browser, found his web server and logged onto email. If the police were savvy enough to monitor his email, they at least wouldn't know where he was when he got online.

Nick closed his eyes to think through what he needed to tell his dad. They had an awkward relationship. Thomas Rail lived for work and didn't make excuses about it. It wasn't that Nick and his dad didn't get along. They just never bothered to try.

He composed the brief 'help me' letter, said he'd get in touch by email and clicked send. Another message flashed onto the screen. Same strange address. Nick read the single line response.

They call me The Moderator.

God help me, Nick thought. A sick feeling swept through his stomach. He fought to steady his fingers and type.

Nick replied. *Okay, what do you want?*

Nick glanced around him. The teller at the register looked his way and picked up a phone. Was she calling him in?

Hurry up, Nick thought. I'm almost out of time.

Nick pulled his pack on and slid to the edge of his seat, waiting for a reply and ready to run. He looked at the cashier. Good. She was talking to a customer.

An email appeared. Nick stared at the monitor, unbelieving.

Give me $100,000, and I'll give you Lana.

The cashier move toward him; Nick scrambled the screen.

"Your time's up. Would you like to buy more time?" she asked.

Nick forced a smile. Relax, he thought. She was just doing her job.

"No thanks. I'm all finished, but do you have any prepaid phones?"

Chapter 62

Lana Summers hadn't seen the man. Maybe he wasn't coming back, yet she expected him to materialize at any moment. She could feel his black hands reaching toward her ...

Thoughts chased each other around her head.

Lana pulled the blanket tighter. The torn fingernail snagged on a fold, sending hot needles of pain up her arm. She fought the urge to throw up again, but there wasn't anything left.

For the first time in her life, Lana knew what it felt like to thirst. The need drove her back to the water.

She lay on the dirt, staring at her dim reflection. She'd managed to pick off bits of crusted blood from her forehead. Her clothes had dried but made the blanket wet. The shivering had stopped for now.

Brown scum covered the rocks lining the pool, but the water lay clear and still. She didn't care what the pool looked like. Lana reached out, dipped her hand in and made the reflection disappear. She scooped freezing water to her mouth and drank greedily.

Funny, she thought. Such sweet water from a gross pool. It settled into the cold place in her middle.

Chapter 63

Preston Farwick logged onto Sonya Hernandez's computer at three a.m. They'd gone out the night before. Another purely platonic meeting, he assured her. He'd dropped her at home, steadied her up to her door and laughed with her as she fumbled the keys. Maybe he'd bought her just one drink too many.

But now he knew she was sleeping off the Friday night happy hour.

Using her IP address was a red herring. If anyone ever tracked the transaction to her computer, she would doubtless check out clear. He could have made the necessary arrangements strictly on the black, but it was, after all, more fun this way.

An online company directory for a shipping and post box company listed branches in all fifty states. Farwick clicked one in Maryland and selected the services he needed. The package would be received, repackaged and forwarded to Sonya's address. He entered his encrypted email so he'd have the tracking numbers.

"God bless the United States Postal Service," he muttered.

Farwick clicked through to the shopping cart, selected VISA and used one of the credit card numbers saved by Sonya's computer. She'd probably contest the charge and the credit card company would eat it.

"Thanks, Ms. Hernandez. You shouldn't have."

Chapter 64

Nick switched off his lights and turned down the quarry lane. He tried not to think about the last time he and Lana had been here. It had been so warm then.

Making the car disappear was no small feat. He'd spent most of the day hiding in a rotting tobacco shed, waiting for dark and studying the map on his new phone. The police would be watching major arteries. Using back roads, farm lanes and even the tracks following power lines, he'd found another way to the quarry.

Nick stopped the car and got out to investigate. He'd never paid much attention to the quarry itself. Lana had been the key attraction.

Scrub trees surrounded the quarry, but a lane cut down from the edge along the far side. Nick followed the lane in the dark, walking carefully and keeping his eyes open. This just might work. Nick stopped where the lane descended into the black water of the swamped quarry. It was hard to imagine that people used to work down there.

He returned to the car, pulled out the back pack and set it by the weed-covered lane. He hated the thought of throwing the car away, but it was a target. Nothing to do about that now. Nick undid the silver snaps that held the convertible cover in place then folded the frame behind the back seat. He didn't bother to fasten it into place before starting the car.

The lane was hard to follow in the dark and Nick was keenly aware of the sound of his exhaust. He did his best to keep the rpm's low. He turned down the track that dipped toward the quarry, switched off the engine and coasted with his foot on the brake. The lane seemed steeper in the car, and he kept his eyes on the drop toward the quarry on his left. This would be easier with lights on, he thought.

Water kissed his tires before Nick ratcheted back on the parking brake. He turned the wheels a little away from the side wall and stood on the driver's seat. He put one foot up on the seat back and reached forward to release the emergency break. As soon as the car started to roll, Nick stepped up over the back seat, onto the trunk and landed in a crouch behind the car.

His red car ambled forward into the water. Bubbles gurgled up from its sides and water sloshed around the air intake before coming level with the front wind screen. The car paused for a moment, as if deciding if it should continue. Nick saw the steering wheel turn and momentum increased. Water swirled up over the sides, pouring around the seats, pulling the vehicle deeper in. It floated. Nick hadn't anticipated that. More black bubbles gurgled around the back wheels, as if the quarry were digesting a meal.

The car sank lower and the chrome bumper hesitated above the water's surface like a grim silver smile before disappearing from view.

A few bubbles marked the spot where it had gone down, but the water soon returned to clean black glass. Nick's scared breathing made frosty bursts in the night air.

Chapter 65

The Moderator watched from his computer at home. Drink, music, and a good movie, he thought. The perfect evening's entertainment. He clicked on the link and waited for the girl to appear on the screen in front of him.

She had moved to the other side of the room. The stone walls didn't make for much variety. She found the blanket and had it wrapped tightly around her. Her face was pretty, even in the infrared green of the night camera.

The Moderator sipped from his glass and zoomed in, studying her. Too young for him, but she didn't know that. He grunted a laugh that brought Cookie's head off the floor.

"I'll bet you've never gone two days without food," he whispered to the screen. "You'll start to notice that tomorrow."

He closed the link and composed an email to Nick with a mailing address. He clicked send and swirled the last of the liquor in his glass. "Show me the money," he muttered.

Chapter 66

Nick gathered brown leaves into a pile for a bed and slept fitfully near the rail line that ran along the river bank. The line crossed the river north of him, slowing to make the corner before entering a short dark tunnel cut through solid rock where the limestone cliffs interfered with the rail line's progress.

He woke long before it arrived. In the near-winter air, the horn sounded long, low and otherworldly. Nick brushed himself off, grabbed his pack and headed for the spot he had picked at the bend on the near side of the tunnel.

It took forever for the freight train to come. Finally, the single white eye of the Diesel engine poked through trees, pointing down at rust-coated rails and driving a hole through the morning river fog. A second engine linked directly behind helped pull the hundred-some cars south. The rumble of the twin, twelve-cylinder engines reverberated in the ground underneath. Just like his bass guitar. He remembered how it felt. He wondered if he'd hear it and feel it again in his butt like he used to when he sat on the amp. He crouched down behind a stand of grass as the train drew alongside.

The engines muffled as they plunged into the tunnel. Time to see if I can still run, Nick thought. He dug his feet into the gravelly earth and eyed a box car near the end.

The engine noise died away on the far side of the cut. Cars clattered on the track nearby. Coal cars, strung like ugly beads on a wire, followed in line, one after the other. Even in the dark, he could see the rounded yellow graffiti spray painted on the side of the three box cars tacked on the end.

Nick ran. The rat tat tat of gravel underfoot mixed with the rattle of the train on track. It started to accelerate; he'd have to hurry. Nick tripped over a discarded tie, swore and scrambled back to his feet. He was sprinting now.

His hands reached out and grasped a cold metal ladder. He pulled, lifting his feet off the ground, clinging to the car seconds before it was swallowed by the tunnel.

Chapter 67

"This is stupid." Darren pushed the papers away from him. "We're not finding anything."

"Sure we have. We've got lots of names," Chase protested.

"What good is that? Names don't tell us anything," Darren stood up, flexing his muscles as he stretched. "We've been at it all day. My parents are going to get home soon, and you all have to clear out."

"Do you have a map?" Ashley asked.

"What kind of a map?"

"A local map. I want to see something," she replied.

Chase stopped what he was doing and looked up. "Great idea. Why didn't I think of that?"

"Because you're not a girl," Ashley wrinkled her nose at him. "Besides, you don't even know what I'm going to do with it."

"I think you're going to find the closest pizza joint. I'm starving," Ralph said.

"How can you think about food while Lana's missing?" Darren asked.

"I'm not; my stomach is thinking about food," Ralph replied.

Darren found a map online. "How big an area do you want?" he asked.

Ashley reached over his shoulder and drew a circle on the screen. He enlarged the map and hit print.

134

Ashley snatched up the paper and set it down next to Chase. "Give me your short list," she demanded.

She started plotting names on the map. "Darren, bring your list over here. You, too, Ralphie."

"That would be Ralph, not Ralphie," he complained.

The others set their lists down and Chase picked up a pen and started helping.

Chapter 68

Freddy Naugle pulled his jeep down the lane and parked next to the derelict silo.

Freddy turned to his friend and killed the engine. "No one ever comes back here."

"Pretty spot. Kind of a shame it's abandoned," Barrett said.

"I'll flush 'em, you drop 'em."

"Deal." Barrett jumped from the jeep and lifted his shotgun from the rack behind their heads.

Freddy zipped his jacket to his chin and pulled on a woolen cap. "I'll start in the barn attic. You set up over there."

"On the front porch?" Barrett raised an eyebrow.

"Why not. It's not like someone is going to come to the front door and complain about the noise. Besides, it'll break the wind." Freddy set off for the barn.

Barrett set a box of shells on a plant stand by the front door.

He squinted up toward the barn roof, estimated where the birds would come out and waited. He bit the glove off his trigger finger hand and dropped it. The glove had barely landed when there was a noise in the barn and the first pigeon exploded through a broken window by the hay loft. Barrett picked his target, leveled the shotgun and followed the line of flight until the tail feathers came into his sights. He kept going, drawing along the line until the sights rested just in front of the bird. He pulled the trigger.

The barrel erupted and the bird crumpled and fell like a wad of paper. A second blast followed and another dropped. Two for two.

#

Lana scrambled to her feet, eyes locked on the door. Again she heard the explosion of sound. Gunshots. Even muted by the earth and stone, she knew they were close. A brief interlude of silence followed. Then more gunshots. She pressed hands over her ears, trying to close it out, trying to gate out the fear.

He was going to kill her today.

Or maybe he was just teasing. Playing with her.

Chapter 69

Nick slipped in behind the box car and settled himself on the step. The temperature and damp river air conspired to make the wind burn his ears, but the platform afforded some protection. He wrapped one arm around an iron brace and curled up as best he could on the metal landing, watching dawn break over southern Pennsylvania as the train continued to pick up speed.

His mind wandered to Lana. The only hope for him was to find her. She could clear his name and tell the police who had taken her.

The rhythmic clacking of the wheels on the track marked time to the endless loop in his mind. Who was The Moderator and where had he taken Lana?

His fingers were too cold to text now. If he dropped the phone, he'd have no way to get in touch with his dad.

Nick could see a long stretch of black river running north, following the line of power stations. All he needed was enough distance to give him some breathing room. The police would clear his record when they found Lana.

The Moderator was after money.

Nick rested his head on his knees. The circle in his mind came unbidden. He didn't bother to fight against it.

The world around him slipped away as he rode the rocking grey hallway. Colors of morning blurred. Sounds slurred.

Somewhere he heard another voice. Hers. He lifted his head but knew he was dreaming. He watched anyway. Lana appeared wearing only shorts and a tee shirt. She must be cold, he thought. Her cheeks and lips were red. Too red. She tried to tell him something, but he couldn't make out the words. Nick squinted past the noise of the train, trying to hear. Nothing. She put a hand on her stomach, then crossed her fingers.

He needed to call to her, reach to her, tell her he would find her. But the anesthesia of sleep numbed his lips. He tried to open his mouth.

The blast of a train whistle erupted from his throat, and Nick snapped awake. His arm had begun to slip and the ties and gravel of the track beneath him flipped past with the staccato of an old film. His mind played the drama of falling underneath the great iron wheels. He shuddered and looked around.

The terrain flattened and the river was gone. Nick stood and stretched, moving his legs and arms alternately. He had to get his blood moving. He peeked around the edge of the box car, looking ahead. A rusting water tower marked the edge of some kind of residential area. He ducked back again, remembering that trains usually had surveillance cameras mounted rear of the engine. The conductor throttled back and the tenor of Diesel engines changed. The coupling underneath Nick shifted as the weight of the cars pushed against the slowing locomotive. Hydraulics hissed and brakes screeched.

Nick moved to the edge of the landing and peeked around. A small stand of trees clumped next to the track before a rail crossing. One of the rail lines that followed him the whole way peeled off from the main and disappeared into the woods. The blue dome of a water tower appear over the trees ahead, and ducked back into his spot as the train crossed a country road. One car sat waiting for the train to pass, but the driver was looking down and didn't notice. Nick needed to get off before his luck ran out.

The train continued to slow and entered a rail cut near a lumber yard. Nick jumped clear of the car and landed hard at the graveled edge of the track. He rolled on the ground and was up and moving before the last car in the consist passed.

Every muscle in his body felt stiff from cold, but he ran until he reached the end of the lumber yard fence. He brushed off his clothes, crossed the street and headed up along the sidewalk. A nearby mill filled the air with the smell of cow feed. A convenience store guarded the corner of the block, but Nick settled on a Laundromat. Besides, it was warm and almost empty. He pushed through the door and sat on a green plastic waiting chair, his back to the glass shop front. The round windows of two washing machines spun blurs of color and suds. One woman across the room folded a pile of clothes into some kind of order. She didn't look up when he came in.

Nick pulled out his phone hoping for something from his dad. He flicked through a few screens and saw another email from The Moderator.

Chapter 70

Thomas Rail planned for Nick to follow him into the business. Nick would start at the bottom like he had and work his way up. Of course, his oversight would make sure Nick got paid more than the rest of the brainless grunts who worked the low level jobs and ensure that promotions came a little faster. Nick wouldn't have to serve much time before moving into one of the regional sales offices. Thomas could pick the territory and decide who he wanted to move in order to make room for his son.

A little red light blinked on the phone at his desk in Austin, Texas. He shut the door and put his son on speaker phone.

"What are you into?"

"I'm not sure," Nick replied. "Lana went out yesterday afternoon and never came back. The police turned up early this morning. They had an email they claimed I wrote asking Lana to meet me last night near Solly's Mart." Nick waited for a response of some kind, then continued. "I ran away."

"You did what?" Thomas couldn't believe his ears.

"They wanted to arrest me again, dad."

"Oh, God." It was a prayer. "You know running is just going to make them think you did it."

"I know. Well, at least I know that now. Just before I left, I got this email from a guy asking if I was looking for Lana. I'd never seen the address before."

"So, we'll just take it to the police."

"He said if I go to the police, Lana will die. If she dies, Dad, then no one will know that I'm innocent. Only her testimony can clear me."

"So what do you need?"

"The guy wants $100,000."

"Holy shit." Thomas Rail stood and walked to the window.

"Yeah. He thinks I stole the money from Seth's grandmother." Nick's voice sounded like plastic in the speaker phone, but he was dead earnest.

"He's barking up the wrong tree. The kid he should talk to is in jail."

"That's what I told him. He doesn't care. He's still got Lana."

"So, where does this guy think you're going to come up with one hundred grand?"

Nick's voice paused on the line, "You."

Chapter 71

Lana's stomach grumbled unhappily. The demon still hadn't returned, but she expected him all the time. The press of hunger drew level with her fear and crowded out the horrible imaginings of what the demon might do when it came back. She even pretended she was baking. She'd never have done that with people watching, but the allure of food was too much. During the day, she stood as much as possible. The stones sucked heat and made her muscles ache. The cold was constant. Unending. Pernicious.

Lana stared at her window. The wavy glass let in an awkward light. Paint peeled around the wooden sash. She studied the wall below it, but the spring pool kept her from getting as close as she wanted. She blew on her fingers and rubbed her hands together, trying to make them feel normal again in spite of the raging pain from the torn nail.

Sequences blurred. Time moved either too fast, or not at all. Lana couldn't tell. The hypothermia started to eat away at her mental acuity. Lana folded the blanket and placed it on the ledge where she was sitting. Flagstones formed the top of the ledge and smaller stones had been stacked on top of each other to form the front. She crouched down next to it and began to pick at one of them, avoiding the use of her throbbing finger.

Bits of dirt gave way between the rock and those around it until it began to wiggle. She stopped and waved her arms around, trying to get the blood back into her fingertips. They began to sting and she kept swinging, trying to ignore the pain. The rock gave her something to do. A way to break the window. A way to let the world out there know where she was. It wasn't much, but it was all she had.

Lana crouched down again and worked. She could smell the stink of her own filth and urine hanging thick in the damp air. Some things were impossible to stop. Lana smiled and glanced at the slippery pile right in front of the doorway. Not exactly a booby trap, but something. It was something.

And it was the 'something's that kept her going; kept her focused. But the cold and fear never left. It was as if she had moved into their room, as if cold and fear lived in this dank springhouse long before she'd ever been shoved inside.

She grasped the edges of the rock, moving it back and forth. She remembered doing the same with her baby teeth. The feel of fingertips on her gums, the gritty sound of it scraping against the teeth next to it.

Lana got down on all fours, face close to the rock. She picked at an embedded pebble, prized it from the crack and wiggled the rock some more. It moved farther this time. More dirt fell out. It was getting looser. Come here, she thought. You don't really want to be in there. "It will only hurt a little," she said.

All I need is a door knob and some dental floss, she thought. Lana sat on the damp floor, put her fingers in around the rock and placed her feet up against the ledge to brace herself. She pulled and her fingers slipped off hard. She rolled back onto the dirt floor, cradling the sore finger against her chest.

She balled her fists, crossed her arms and waited for the stinging to stop. Returning to her spot she brushed away a fresh spill of black earth, the fruit of her last effort.

Then she pushed her tingling fingers in as far as they would go. The rock slid easily toward her and landed on her lap. Another flush of earth followed, covering her legs with damp dirt. She could feel the moisture taking heat from her legs, but she didn't care. She had the rock.

Lana stood up, feeling the heft of her prize. It would work. It was heavy.

144

The light seemed to call to her from the window. Maybe she could go home today, eat something, take a warm bath and try to feel safe again.

The square mirror of the spring pool separated her from the window. She raised the rock in her right hand, steadying it with the other, like a shot put. She'd seen them do it all the time at track. Lana closed her eyes, trying to remember their form. How they crouched before they threw it. Nothing. She couldn't remember any more. Her brain worked slower than normal; the cold nibbled at her mind like a computer virus.

She took a breath. Took aim. Coiled her body back on itself. Untwisting, she forced the rock up toward the target. She saw it leave her finger tips, saw it flash for a second across the grey square of light. She watched it smash hopelessly into the wall beneath the window and fall. The spring pool shattered with its impact. She stood staring, trying to see the rock she'd rescued from the wall, the rock that failed her.

She became vaguely aware of an exhausted feeling in her body. Her hungry muscles ached for food and rest. Warm tears tickled her face and that part, at least, felt good because the shivering had returned.

Chapter 72

Lori Summers sat in the conference room of the Trent Police Department. She hadn't bothered to hide her bags and lines and flat hair. Nothing mattered. She ate when she had to. But most times she ended up sticking her fingers far back on her tongue until the undigested food splashed past her hand into the toilet while she knelt there, berating herself for eating when her own daughter was still missing. When Lana was still some place where strange hands did anything they wanted to her.

Lori shuddered and picked at the Formica peeling from the table's edge. A door opened and Ron entered with Officer Sinclair. Ron's pale, drawn face didn't bother to smile. He finally looked human. The facts were too much for him, too.

"Thanks for coming," Sinclair dropped a thin file on the desk and sat down. "I'll be as direct as possible."

Lori nodded. She pressed toes together under the table and folded her hands. Get on with it.

"Nick evaded arrest. It's a dead giveaway that he was involved. Exactly how, we don't know."

He touched the folder, but didn't bother to open it.

"What are the odds?" Ron asked.

Of course, Lori thought. Of course he would ask that.

"I don't much like the feel of raw statistics. There are too many variables," Sinclair sidestepped the question.

"Just give me a number, officer," Ron pressed.

"Lana has been missing for almost seventy-two hours. That's a long time," Sinclair said.

"What does that mean?" Lori couldn't help herself.

"Miss Summers. We're not done here. Even as we speak, there are officers looking for Lana and Nick Rail. They're not going to let up."

"So where does that leave us?" Ron asked.

Sinclair squared off with the girl's father. "Ninety-two percent of kids who have been abducted are found within seventy-two hours. Almost fifty percent of them are found in the first three."

"That's not good, is it," Lori started picking at the table edge again.

"No." Sinclair said, "It isn't good."

Chapter 73

Nick pulled on a green ball cap and sorted the money in his pack. He had been too long in the Laundromat, and it was time to hit the street. He bought a coffee and an egg sandwich from a dumpy diner and ate while he walked. He fought to keep his mind clear and thinking. The lumberyard and feed mill were the only real businesses in town. The broken hand rails, cracked plastic porch furniture and faded green shutters reminded him of Seth's trailer park. The best looking homes had fresh paint and for-sale signs.

Nick slipped past a shop and small town sheriff's office, turned down an alley and followed it past rusting chain link fences until he reached a post office. A young woman pulled up and parked along the curb. She wore medical scrubs with pink and purple polka dots. Nick watched her walk into the post office. Through the window he saw her stop in front of a wall of boxes. Letter-sized brass doors with glass windows. He looked back at her car. Still running.

Nick checked the alley and walked toward it. No one knew he was here. He could put more distance between himself and trouble.

He saw his reflection in the paint and decided to keep walking. He didn't need to give police another reason to follow him.

Nick shuffled down the road, waiting for his phone to ring. The houses on this end of town were better kept. A square brick elementary school dominated the far side of the block. A few kids attempted a poor game of four-square with a green plastic ball. They didn't notice him. He should be in school, too.

Nick stood a little straighter and headed toward a church. A few black spotted pumpkins sat on an untidy hay bale just off the main entrance. He climbed the stairs and tried the brass handle. It was open.

The foyer smelled of cold coffee, old women and older books. The church wasn't as warm as the Laundromat but it was still better than outside. Paper signs taped to the wall pointed to the prayer chapel. Nick stood by the doors to the main sanctuary. The paper sign read, 'Always open.'

Nick went in and sat in the back row. Nick's family didn't do the church-thing. His mom watched one of those loud preachers on cable every now and then, but he never paid much attention to it.

The quiet of the sanctuary, though unfamiliar, seemed strangely intimate, as if God were waiting for him to say something.

He looked around again. No one else was waiting to talk to God, so he figured it wouldn't hurt to try.

A large cross supported an ivory colored Jesus. Jesus's head hung off to one side. Nick cleared his throat and tried to figure out what to say.

"Can I help you?" Nick startled. A man smiled at him from the aisle.

"Are you real?" Nick asked.

"Of course. Why?"

"Because you just appeared there. Freaky." Nick said. The man wore a coarse brown robe with a rope belt. Probably a monk or something, Nick reasoned.

"Sorry. I didn't mean to surprise you. Are you here for prayer?"

Nick looked back at the too-white-Jesus. "Yes. I mean, I guess so. I've never really tried it before."

"I see." The man didn't seem concerned that Nick hadn't ever bothered with God. "Is there something in particular on your mind?"

Nick grimaced. "It's kind of complicated. I've got a friend who's in trouble. I'm worried about her."

He nodded. "Why don't we start up there?"

Nick followed the robe down the aisle. Empty wooden pews reached away from him to paintings that dominated the side walls. Tall men with colored robes and pale, yellow halos. But the colors blued and their feet had faded where people had brushed up against them over the years.

The monkish man stopped at a short column with a metal basin. Dipping a finger in the water, he made the sign of the cross.

He led Nick to a sand table set off to the side. Several old candle ends remained where they had burned out.

"Sometimes, when I don't have words, I light a candle," he said. "The candle is a symbol of my request. It's a way to give my problem to God." He gave Nick a candle that smelled like honey.

Nick followed the man's lead and pressed Lana's candle into the sand. The man lit his and handed Nick the matches.

Nick watched the flame travel from his match to the waxy tip. The fire rose thin and unwavering.

Chapter 74

Ashley and Chase entered the last dot on the map and sat back, admiring their work.

"Take a look at this, Ralph," Chase said.

Ralph leaned over Ashley's shoulders. The names and locations for the seventeen-plus cases he'd hacked out of the juvenile court records clustered almost exclusively around Florin, Morris and Trent. "That looks like the freaking Bermuda Triangle," he said. "If you ignore the outliers, almost everything falls in this sector."

Darren joined them and eyed the map. "Now what?"

"I don't think we're going to get any closer unless we have access to the kids' computers," Ralph said.

"What kids?" Darren asked.

"The kids whose files we pulled."

"You pulled," Ashley reminded.

"Whatever," Ralph ignored her.

"So who would have those?"

"Morris and Trent share a police department. Florin has their own."

"Wait." Ralph help up a finger. "I know a police officer in Florin."

"You know him?" Ashley asked.

"Yeah, he's my neighbor. He's cool. He keeps his pool open for us over the summer."

"You think he's The Moderator?" Darren asked.

Ralph laughed. "Officer Dixon? Hell no. He doesn't know shit about computers. But he did say they hired a cyber-detective to help them with all this stuff."

"He's not doing very well," Ashley said.

"That's because their cyber guy needs this," Chase waved the map.

"What do you mean?" she asked.

"He probably isn't allowed to dig through juvenile records either," Chase gathered up the papers. "Maybe they can for a kid they're tracking down, but not more than that."

"Why not?" Darren asked.

"Because this is America. We have rights," Chase replied.

"Great. So all Ralph has to do is walk over there and tell them he's hacked into the county court house?" Ashley said.

"I could tell Officer Dixon that someone else did it," Ralph tried. "I don't have to tell them who. I can show them the name clusters and ask him to have their cyber guy take a look at it."

"Why would they listen to you, anyway?" Ashley asked.

"Because Lana's missing," Chase replied. "We've narrowed down the whereabouts of The Moderator to three towns. We've got a few dozen names. Most of them are police officers. If we take them out of the picture, there aren't many names left." Chase was thinking aloud. "This might give them the leads they need to find Lana."

"Wait. Let me go pack my bag. At least then I'll be ready when they come to haul us off to jail," Ashley replied tartly.

"We could use the necessity defense," Chase suggested.

"Right, Chase. The *necessity* defense." Ashley scowled. "And what the hell is that?"

"Basically it's the idea that you can break a law if you're trying to save a life. I read it somewhere."

"You should get out more," Ashley said.

"You think it will work?" Darren asked.

"There's only one problem," Chase said. "Ralph hacked in before Lana went missing."

"We're screwed," Ashley said.

Chapter 75

Lana couldn't make the shivering stop. It felt worse than the hunger. She pulled the blanket tighter and pressed herself into the corner. It helped some, but the rock underneath stole her heat. She felt like a tire that wouldn't hold air anymore.

The light in the window started to fade long before she was ready. The nights weren't much colder, but the fear and hunger crowded closer in the darkness. She got up. Her muscles ached. Or maybe it was her bones. Her feet had stayed wet the longest and now she couldn't feel them at all. She tied her shoes tighter after falling in the water, thinking that might keep them warmer.

Lana pulled them up on the ledge beside her and rubbed them through the canvas of her shoes. Couldn't feel that either.

She stumbled to the front door, avoiding the pile and reached over the spring pool to run her hand over the wall. Her sore finger bumped against the rock and she winced. If she could climb the wall, she might be able to break the window. She *had* to break the window and at least hang her arm out, maybe wave someone down. If there was anyone there.

Chapter 76

The monk left, and Nick watched the wick burn wax down to a sputtering lump in the sand. He picked up a candle snuffer and dropped the bell over the flame. He put the snuffer back and watched the straight silver ribbon of smoke rise into the room.

Nick moved back to a pew, opened his phone and ran through the drill of becoming invisible before getting on line. He didn't know who was watching, and he sure as hell didn't want to give himself away before he got Lana back.

There was a 'call me' email from his dad. He hadn't expected to hear from him this soon.

Nicked dialed the number, and his father picked up on the second ring.

"Hey, dad."

"I have the money together."

"Thank God." Nick paused. "How do we know the guy will tell me where Lana is after you give him the money?" He voiced the obvious question.

"Well, based on what you're telling me, we don't have much choice." His father grew quiet on the other end. "I sure hope this works. If it doesn't, you'll just have to turn yourself in."

"I can't do that, dad." Nick closed his eyes. "I don't want to go back there. No one will believe me. Especially after what happened with Seth."

"We'll, let's not worry about that yet. You keep your head down, and I'll send off the cash to the address you've been given."

"Dad," Nick struggled to find the words. He'd never really talked to his dad before. Not like this. "I'm scared." It felt good to say it aloud.

A silence hung over the line. He heard his father listening to it as well, heard the little scratching noises his face made against the phone. Nick went on. "I'm afraid we won't find Lana." Nick swallowed. "I'm afraid of going to jail, of ending up like Seth. Locked away forever."

"I won't let that happen, Nick. You're a good boy. Remember that."

His father hung up and Nick sat staring at the phone.

Then Nick clicked on the last email from The Moderator, hit reply and typed: *The money is on its way. ETA tomorrow at noon.*

He included his phone number as instructed.

Nick clicked send and shoved the phone back into his pocket.

Chapter 77

Sonya Hernandez curled on the corner of her couch watching the news. Another early snow storm hammered New York City. Her feet burrowed under the cushion next to her. Another night at home alone. Maybe she should just get a dog. At least then someone might be waiting for her after work.

She sipped hot cocoa from a flowered mug and picked up the television remote. A man appeared; someone she recognized. A police officer. She'd probably seen him in the court house or maybe at a party. His title flashed across the screen. Officer Sinclair. She didn't recognize the name. The reporter's voice-over stopped and the officer read a prepared statement. A young girl, Lana Summers was listed as missing. Sonya shook her head. Too much like work. She pushed the button and the screen went black.

Sonya pulled the sofa blanket over her legs. A dog would be nice; she could take it running.

Then she thought of having to leave it at home while she worked. Maybe her boss would let the dog come to work. . .

Right. Fat chance.

Her phone buzzed on the coffee table. Preston Farwick's name flashed on the screen. She stared at the phone and tapped her finger nails on the mug, watching it ring. Why did all the nice guys have to be married? She didn't care if he was a little older. What did that matter? Really. She just wanted someone to curl up next to on the couch. Someone who would tuck the blanket in around her feet and share her cocoa and talk. Someone who might bring a little purpose to cooking. She was tired of cooking for one.

The phone stopped vibrating. She ignored it, turned her cocoa mug on its side. Using her fingers she scooped out a half-melted marshmallow and licked it off. He'd left a message.

Sonya sighed and reached for the phone.

Chapter 78

Preston Farwick opened the camera link to the girl. It looked like she hadn't moved. The resolution was bad, especially at night, but the thermal quality of his infrared optics was exceptional. She wasn't as bright as she had been yesterday.

He moused over the girl's chest. A pop-up floated a temperature reading over the spot.

Preston Farwick sat up straighter and checked a few more spots.

"Getting a little cold, are we?" He set his cup down and peered at the screen. Her body temperature was dropping.

He leaned back again, crossed his arms, and stared. The thermal camera displayed no reds. Her hands and legs showed a cold dark blue. A light green spread across her abdomen and yellow curled around her neck, but no red.

"Your boyfriend had better hurry up, or you won't be around to celebrate being found," Farwick smiled at his own joke.

He entered a command string. The spring-house door unlocked remotely. The girl stirred at the noise, but didn't get up.

Chapter 79

Seth Mallory stood on the corner of the metal bunk shelf facing the wall of his cell. A pair of khaki shorts hung just below his hip bones, but his pale blue tee shirt lay in a wad on the floor next to his mattress. Seth reached above his head. A guitar tattoo floated on his skin as his shoulder blade rose and fell. He drew another tiny circle onto the five line staff of the treble clef.

Seth tucked the pencil behind his ear and stood back on the bunk. The five-line grand staff ran the full length of the wall above his bed. Bass and treble clef joined by a brace.

The only problem is he couldn't whistle both lines at once, but he could hear it in his mind.

Seth jumped down from the bunk, pulled on his shirt and shoved the mattress back on the bunk shelf. The score lay perfectly straight across the wall. He'd managed using only the edge of the five-inch New Testament a prison chaplain had given him.

He stood back. The angry punk rock he used to hear in his head had faded. This song floated through his mind with a strangely Celtic feel. The sound of sadness. Loss.

And beauty. Yes. That was it, Seth decided. Beauty.

Chapter 80

"Nick ran away," Darren said.

"I know," Ashley threw her coat on the chair. "I heard."

"We've got to take our analysis in to the police," Chase said.

Ralph swore under his breath several times before voicing up. "I'll do it," he said, resigned. "I know Officer Dixon, so it might as well be me."

"What are you going to give him?" Chase asked.

Ralph shrugged. "Everything. I'll burn it on a CD and take it over."

"You're a hacker, Ralphie. I didn't think you believed in using front doors," Ashley replied.

"There's a first time for everything, right?" He shrugged.

"No, Ralphie," Darren stood up. "I'm taking it in."

"Why you?"

"Because, I owe something." He glanced at Ashley. "It's the least I could do. Besides, my parents have enough money to hire lawyers if I get in a jam."

Ralph waited for Darren to change his mind. "Fine," he said. "I'll bring it to school tomorrow."

Chapter 81

Lana stumbled across the floor and reached for the wall. In the growing delirium of hypothermia, she couldn't remember what day it was or how long the sun had been up. But the light from the window called to her, drew her in. She needed to break the glass, but she wasn't sure why. Try as she might, she couldn't make her mind tell her why. She blinked again, trying to focus. Climb the wall, she thought. Break the glass.

A ledge above the pool ran under the window. She slid out; her hands groped for holds along the bare stones. Her sore finger stood awkwardly back. She found a hold. Nose to stone she shuffled her wooden feet onto the ledge. At least she could still stand on them. She moved further. A loose stone dropped into the pool behind her. The pool wasn't deep. Three feet maybe. Lana craned her neck, looking up. The window hung like a pale sun, directly above her. She took a breath, and began to climb. A crevice here for her right foot. She pushed up with her leg, reaching above for more.

It was working. She was getting higher. Lana turned her face to the side, cold rock on her cheek, pulling herself up. Almost to the window sill. She looked for a toe hold. Her feet didn't feel anything.

Desperate fingers reached the lip of the sill, pulling again. Swinging feet searched for a new place to stand.

They found something. Her face rose level with the glass. The shivering threatened her grip. She fought against it, lifted one hand free and smashed it through the glass. A rush of wind pushed past her face. She clung there, staring at the fractured window. Beyond that bare trees and green firs spread to the right and left. She couldn't see anything else. Freedom was so close.

Blood oozed from a jagged cut on the back of her hand. She could see something white inside. Must be deep.

She should take care of that, but the notion seemed distant, unimportant. She shifted her feet to crane her head close to the window.

The toehold on her right foot gave way. The square of light moved away from her. The wall pulled back from her as she fell. Hands clawed uselessly at air.

Water engulfed her. Swallowed her. Merciless icy fingers groped under her clothes surrounding her skin. Lana gasped, eyes wide, choking water.

Muscles seized and cramped. A single point of thought ruptured through the haze of Lana's mind. She twisted her core, felt slippery stones under her, sat up and rolled, throwing her arms over the side and pulled herself from the death pool, up onto the dirt floor.

Lana heard a clattering sound. At first she thought of horses. Maybe it was someone banging at the door. Then she realize it was her own teeth. Too cold.

So tired. She managed to pull her knees up. She needed to sleep. Just a little nap, she thought.

Just a little nap. The hypnotic, deadly sleep of hypothermia.

Lana blinked. Nick and Seth walked in with their guitars. Nick was smiling. How could he be here? Her brain refused to answer the question. She waved, but Nick didn't see her. They plugged in and began to play. Lana sang along, her childlike voice joining the hallucination. She wanted to dance, but someone had tied her feet. She called to Nick; he didn't respond. He wouldn't stop playing.

"Please Nick, dance with me?" She reached out to him, and he disappeared. She was surrounded, once again, by stone and dirt and darkness.

Chapter 82

Sonya opened at the knock. Preston Farwick waited in a grey woolen overcoat and leather gloves.

"Sure is getting cold," he said by way of a hello.

"Come in." She stood aside, smelling the familiar lime and sage of his cologne.

"Thanks for letting me ship that package here. The wife already thinks I spend too much money on computer stuff."

She turned to the table and lifted the dense, brown-paper parcel addressed to Preston Farwick, care of her own address. "Here you go."

"Will you let me buy you drink?" he asked hopefully.

She sighed and smiled. "Is that what this is all about?"

"Was I that obvious?" He reached up and tucked a loose tendril of hair behind her ear. The finger slid the length of her neck.

Sonya looked away and wondered about his wife. "Preston, I need to stop seeing you." She put a finger on his lips to stop the protest.

He kissed the finger. "Why?"

"Because I like you." Her hand dropped to fiddle with his coat toggles.

"I thought that was the idea."

"That's *not* the idea. That's the problem." She pulled her hand away.

"How is that a problem?"

"Listen, you're a great guy. But you have a big problem."

"Let me guess. I'm too old for you? That it?"

"No, Preston. You're married. That's the big problem. Maybe that doesn't bother you, but it bothers me. A lot. Why should I play with what I can never have?"

"Who says you can't?" Preston's fingers lingered on the skin of her shoulder.

"Me. I don't want to share a man."

Farwick nodded slowly and turned away.

Sonya stepped up behind him and put a hand on the arm cradling the brown package. He turned. She tried to read his face.

"Preston. Thanks for telling me the truth about you." She reached up and kissed him; her lips lingered on his. She could taste her own tears in the kiss. Maybe he could, too. Then she pulled away.

"Goodbye." He walked down the stairs and didn't look back.

Sonya Hernandez pushed the door shut against the cold.

Chapter 83

Freddy loaded his gun and waited. Barrett walked toward the barn. His turn to flush first. The pigeons were endless. They'd both conspired to get off work early so they could get back here.

"Hey, Freddy."

"Yeah?"

"What do you make of that?" Barrett stood at the corner of the barn and pointed down toward the spring house.

"It's a spring house."

"No, I mean next to it?" Barrett moved toward the spring house then started running.

"Holy cow." Freddy squinted, leaned his gun against the wall and ran after his friend.

Barrett got there first. He was on his knees as Freddy ran up. "What the hell?"

The girl's hair was black, but the rest of her was some shade of blue. "She's soaked and she's hypothermic," Barrett replied. He checked for a pulse. "Oh God. Get the blanket from the jeep and call 911."

Freddy stood staring. Eyes wide. Barrett saw his friend hadn't moved. He swung a weak punch at the man and shouted, "Move. I need it right now."

Freddy turned. His hunting boots hammered back up the path.

Barrett sucked in the cold air and held it. Letting it warm in his lungs. Then he leaned over, put his lips against the girl's. He pinched her nose and breathed the warm air into her cold lungs. Gently now.

Again. He held a breath. Counted slowly to ten and pushed the warm air inside her. He could hear Freddy running behind him. Another breath. Slow and steady. Freddy slid in beside them. The girl's face hadn't changed.

Chapter 84

Nick Rail walked out of town after leaving the church and wondered along the railroad tracks. Too much time in town and folks would start asking questions. He shivered and turned up his coat collar against the wind.

His phone vibrated. Nick quickly fumbled it from his pocket. A text. The number was listed as 'unknown'. He tapped the screen. Nick turned and started running back toward town. His pack bounced along behind and his lungs burned.

The Moderator had actually sent an address.

Nick jumped over a low spot on the fence, sprinted through the lumber yard and across the street toward the sheriff's office.

He burst in the front door. "Please help. I know where she is." He was talking before he reached the counter.

The receptionist removed a pair of half glasses, put her hand on his. "Calm down, son. What can we do for you?"

"It's my girlfriend. She was kidnapped in Pennsylvania. The guy who did it just sent me the address where she's being kept."

"What's her name?" The woman keyed in the name and put her glasses back on to read the screen. Nick anticipated having to do more explaining.

"Lana Summers," she slipped him a piece of paper. "Give me the address."

Nick turned on his phone and wrote, fighting with cold fingers to keep it legible.

The woman entered the information and labeled it 'top priority.'

"And you are?" the woman asked.

"I'm Nick Rail."

She nodded. Glanced back at the screen. A frown creased her face. "Looks like you had better stay with me, then."

"Are you arresting me?" Nick asked.

"Yes, I am."

"I didn't do it, you know. Are you going to put on handcuffs?"

"Do I need to?" She peeked over the top of her glasses. Eyebrows up.

"No, ma'am."

"Good, then have a seat over there. I'll get you some coffee. We'll wait for the sheriff to come back from his meeting. Then we'll drive you home."

"Can I just get a cab? I have to see her."

"No need." She pointed through the window. "He just came in."

Chapter 85

Dispatch received the call and scrambled emergency and police to the address. The ambulance people had to wait until police cleared the scene. They had no idea what they might find.

Sinclair glanced at his GPS and punched on lights and siren. He couldn't help but see the faces of his own girls. Screw regulations, he thought, and picked up speed. He knew these roads and he needed to get there.

The ground pulled away from the cruiser as he flashed over a knoll. Five miles from the destination.

He pushed his radio button. "Dispatch, please notify the family that rescue is in progress."

God, let me have good news to tell. He glanced in his rear view and saw another cruiser gaining on him. Pay day, he thought. Let's go get her, boys. Cars pulled off to the side as they sailed past. Radio chatter increased as emergency personnel went live. A volunteer fireman blocked cross traffic on the intersection ahead, his hand waving him through. The stop sign flashed past. Two miles.

Sinclair could see an ambulance across the fields, running to the same point of intersect, and he completed a pat-check. Kevlar vest. Weapon.

Another cruiser joined the convoy. Three blue and whites—all lights and noise and hurry-up. They sped through another intersection blocked by another fireman.

How did these guys get here so fast? Thank God for volunteers.

The calm GPS announced, "You have reached your destination." Sinclair flew past the waiting ambulance. "You have reached your destination."

A civilian vehicle blocked the farm lane.

Chapter 86

The small-town sheriff chatted non-stop on the drive back to Trent. Nick sat in the back of the cruiser willing him to go faster. He had no idea how far he'd come on the train, and it took much longer to get back than he thought.

They re-crossed the cold, black Susquehanna River and took the first exit for Trent.

"Where are we going?" Nick asked.

"To the Trent police station." The sheriff glanced in the rearview at him. A thick security shield separated Nick from the officer. "There is a warrant out for your arrest."

"Did they find Lana?"

"I'm not sure."

"Can I see her?"

"Son. Right now they think you kidnapped her. Until that assumption changes, you can expect to see very little of anyone."

"But I didn't do it." Nick felt sick. I didn't do it, he thought.

"Well, according to my reports, you ran away from the officer who served the initial warrant." The sheriff turned at a light. "That doesn't look too good, son."

Nick glanced at the eyes in the rearview mirror. "I know."

Chapter 87

"Get her clothes off." Barrett wasn't asking.

Freddy made a face. "Really?"

"Look. She's losing heat faster than she's taking it in. If we don't get her out of this wet stuff, we might as well start digging a hole for her body."

Freddy untied the girl's shoes while Barrett tore open the girl's shirt and rolled her over to pull it off. He unfolded the blanket, lay it on the ground, rolled her back onto it and draped the rest over her.

Freddy fiddled with the girl's pants button. "This feels all wrong."

"Use your knife. Cut 'em off. Just get it done. We don't know how long she's been like this." Barrett held another breath and breathed it into her. He could feel the girl's body jerking as his friend cut the pants free. Barrett shoved his own blaze orange hunting cap down over the girl's head, covering her eyes, ears and most of her nose.

"Why don't we get her into the truck. It's warm in there." Freddy talked while he dialed 911.

"Not yet. If her outsides warm up faster than her insides, it might kill her." Barrett held his breath and filled the girl's lungs again.

Sirens sailed across the meadow. Freddy looked from his phone to the road. "Shit, your fast!" he said to the operator. "The ambulance is here already."

"Stay with me girl." Barrett said, "Stay with me." He paused to tuck the blanket a little tighter. "I'm getting dizzy. Your turn. Take a breath.

Count to ten to warm it up. Then put it in. Don't forget to hold her nose."

Freddy dropped the phone, ignoring questions from the emergency operator. He held his breath and followed his friend's example.

Barrett saw the spring house door standing open. The girl must have dragged herself out. What the hell was she doing in there in the first place? "God, don't let her die."

After ten rounds, Barrett took over again, watching the girl's chest rise as he exhaled.

Chapter 88

Sinclair piled from the cruiser and crouched behind his open door, gun aimed toward the jeep. He motioned for another officer. The man ran, crouching, toward the empty vehicle, weapon ready. Gun racks hung over the back seat. Other officers fanned out around the house.

"Over here." A voice called from beyond the barn. "Down there."

Sinclair ran to the sound. Two men knelt over something in the meadow.

There was nothing for cover between here and there. "Let's go. Three officers followed Sinclair down the slope toward the men.

"Police. Put your hands in the air," Sinclair shouted

The men didn't respond and Sinclair soon saw why. He called in the EMT's. He looked toward the spring house and waved the other officers over to check it out.

He knelt down opposite the stranger. "I know CPR. Ready. Switch." Time to give the man a break. The girl's breathing was shallow, but she was still unresponsive.

"Name's Barrett. Just found her. Been going for four or five minutes now."

Barrett knelt back and Sinclair took turns giving chest compressions.

Sinclair worked and Barrett talked to the EMT's. "Do you have heated oxygen?"

They looked at him strangely.

"Look. I used to live in Canada. She's in the advanced stages of hypothermia. I've seen it before. You can help me or do it your way. If you do it your way, she's probably going to die."

"No." The EMT made his choice. "We only have regular oxygen tanks."

"Get 'em," Barrett barked.

"Let's move her up to the truck," the EMT suggested.

"Not yet." Barrett had taken charge. This was his girl. He gave them a withering glare. "Get the oxygen. Just drive the truck down here. I need more blankets."

Sinclair kept going with CPR and Barrett pulled a heat pack from his pocket. They were perfect for keeping fingers warm while hunting.

The ambulance rattled down the lane. The headlights made shadows of the men. A green oxygen tank appeared next to Barrett. He tore open the heat pack and wrapped the clear plastic oxygen hose around it as many times as it would allow. Then he wrapped the whole business in a foil emergency blanket from the ambulance.

The EMT's found more blankets and lay these under and over the girl.

Barrett held the mask with warmed oxygen over the girl's face. "Nice and easy now," he said.

Chapter 89

Lori Summers and her ex-husband waited on opposite sides of the hospital room. Ron's new wife flipped aimlessly through a fashion magazine. What a bitch, Lori thought. She bit her tongue and felt rage pound in her ears.

No one spoke. The horror of waiting morphed into something worse. More immediate. The threat of finality.

A door opened and a man with a white lab coat appeared. "I can take you back now."

"How is she?" Lori asked.

"She's still unresponsive. Her blood sugar was very low. That just exacerbated the impact of the hypothermia. She probably didn't have anything to eat in the last three days, but the baby is fine."

"Excuse me?" Lori stared blankly at the doctor. Ron shot Lori a glare.

"Sorry. I'm guessing by your reaction that you didn't know about this." He looked at the three parents. Just speak plainly, he'd been told. "Lana is about twelve weeks pregnant."

Lori didn't want to admit she knew nothing about it. Her daughter didn't hide things from her. Lori nodded. "Good." It was the appropriate Catholic response.

Ron muttered something under his breath about Lana being a pitiful excuse for a mother. Lori ignored the comment. They followed the lab coat down a tiled hallway and through two pairs of swinging doors. He stopped before they entered the room. "Don't expect too much. We

178

have no way of knowing how long the coma will last. It's different for everyone."

Chapter 90

Thomas Rail met his son in the station interview room. It wasn't déjà vu. A guard stood at the doorway, pretending not to listen. His son looked tired. Worn from days of hiding and running.

"I'm glad you called me." Thomas choked on the words.

"How is she, dad?"

Thomas blinked hard and drew a little circle on the table with his finger. "Not good, Nick. She slipped into a coma after they got her to the hospital."

"What does that mean?" Nick asked.

"I'm not sure."

"Really?"

"Well, there's a chance she might not wake up."

"No." Nick put his head down on the table and locked his fingers in his hair. His knuckles went white, fighting against the grief. Not wanting to let it out. Not wanting to admit it might be over.

Thomas just watched. Didn't reach out to him.

He went on. "Her parents are pressing charges."

Nick lifted his head. "What? How can they? I didn't do anything, Dad."

Thomas cleared his throat. "They have evidence; it's compelling." His fingers stopped. "The email. The fact that mom was in the shower

when the abduction occurred. We can't vouch for you being at home."
He paused. Looked away. "There are also reports that your vehicle was
spotted near the farm at around that time."

"How is that possible?" Nick's lip began to tremble.

"They have these anonymous tip hotlines. Someone called in a vehicle
with your description."

"There are other cars just like it, dad. You know that."

Thomas didn't answer.

"Then we'll just have to hope Lana wakes up."

Chapter 91

The Moderator reached behind him and clicked play. Chopin. Always Chopin. Unlike the Polish composer, Farwick thought, I will die with money to spare. Preston Farwick slipped his fingers under the tape and peeled back the brown paper. Inside was another box, bearing a different address. Farwick wadded the first round of paper and dropped it into the bin.

He lifted a silver-handled letter opener and slipped the blade under the seams of the package. The box lid opened. Farwick lay the blade back in its cradle and lifted the cash from the box.

He held the cash to his face and breathed in, eyes closed.

"What do you think of that, Cookie?" Farwick held the bundle of cash out to his dog. "Not bad for a day's work, eh?"

Chapter 92

Lori adjusted her tired body in the plastic recliner next to Lana's bed. Her daughter looked so perfect. Her color had improved. The blue around her lips stayed the longest, but now that had all but faded.

Ron went back to work. No surprise there. He'd never really been involved anyway. Even when they lived in the same house. Now his only input was criticism and a monthly check mandated by the courts.

Lori stood and leaned over her daughter. "Lana, honey. It's your mom." She looked so young. Too young.

Lori turned and sat on the edge of the bed, staring through Venetian blinds at the roof of another hospital wing.

"Where's Nick?"

Lori snapped around. "Lana! Oh, thank God you're awake." She pushed the girl's hair back and stroked her face.

"What happened? Where's Nick?"

Awareness dawned. "Oh, honey. Nick is in jail. He can't hurt you now. You're safe here."

Lana looked confused. "Why is he in jail? Where am I?"

"You're in the hospital, Lana. You almost died from the cold. I can't believe Nick would do that to you."

"Do what?" Lana asked. The fog still hadn't lifted. "I'm so thirsty."

Lori's eyes flitted toward her daughter's abdomen and back. She held a bottle with a plastic straw for Lana. "Don't worry about it, dear. I'll take care of you now."

"I want to see Nick." Lana formed the words slowly.

"Honey. What are you talking about? Nick tried to kill you. He locked you up and left you for dead." Lori could feel the rage. The same rage she felt for Ron when she found him with another woman.

"Nick didn't do that, mom."

"Of course he did. He sent you that email and you went to meet him. Then he took you to that farm and—"

"No, mom. That wasn't Nick."

"What?"

"It was some old guy with dreadlocks."

"Dreadlocks?"

"Yes. He was black."

Lori shook her head. Trying to take it in. Hunting over the puzzle to make the pieces match. She began to assimilate Lana's words. "Oh dear."

Chapter 93

Officer Sinclair stepped into the elevator and pressed the button. It would be nice to speak to the girl he'd spent so much time tracking down. Cases like these didn't often have a happy ending.

He watched the red numbers climb to six. The elevator dinged. He followed signs to room 323. Sinclair knocked.

Lori pulled the door open and smiled. The drawn look around the woman's face had disappeared though the shadow of sleepless nights still lingered beneath her eyes. "Come in. Lana's awake now."

"Thank you." He walked to the foot of her bed and marveled at the girl's improved color. "You look much better when you're not some shade of blue." He held out a hand. "I'm Officer Sinclair."

"Lana, this is the police officer whose job it was to find you." Lori didn't elaborate, remembering her own harsh words.

"Hi," the girl answered shyly. "Thanks, I guess."

"You are most welcome. I'm just glad that you are safe." Sinclair looked across at the girl's mother. "Your mother said you're ready to make a statement?"

"Yes. I think so."

"You sure?" Sinclair looked at the girl's cobalt eyes. They seemed tired.

"Yes. I'm ready."

"I'm afraid I'm going to have to ask you some pretty uncomfortable questions. That okay?"

Lana nodded. He pulled a notebook from his pocket and clicked open a pen. "We don't have to do this all at once. You let me know when you're tired. We don't have to finish today."

"Why don't you start by telling me what happened. I'd like to record this if that's okay with your mom."

Lori nodded.

Lana began with her conversation with Nick. Her soft voice walked through all the details. She didn't flinch when she mentioned the baby, though she did glance at her mother and apologize.

Lana mentioned the email she thought was from Nick and told Sinclair about the man behind Solly's Mart.

"How old a man was he?" Sinclair asked.

"I don't know. Fifty maybe?" she answered.

"What did his voice sound like?"

"What do you mean?"

"Was there anything that stood out about his voice? Did he seem well spoken or have an accent? That kind of thing."

Lana thought this over. "I think he had an accent. Kind of a southern sound, but I'm not sure."

"What did he look like?"

"He was dressed in coveralls, like a janitor. He was sweeping. I didn't really stop to think why anyone would bother to sweep behind a store."

186

She bit her lip remembering the conversation. She didn't want to tell the officer that the man said Nick wanted him to pick her up. Her mom had said Nick was in jail because of this. "He had long black dreadlocks with one of those funny knit hats on top. And sunglasses. Big ones."

Sinclair took notes. Lana kept talking.

A nurse breezed into the room to check Lana's vitals. Sinclair moved back against the wall to get out of her way.

The nurse turned and shook a finger at the officer. "This young lady needs to get some rest."

Sinclair smiled. "Yes, she does. I think we're just about done."

#

"I'll walk you out," Lori offered.

They stepped into the hallway and ambled past the nurses' station.

"I think I owe you an apology," Lori said. "I haven't exactly been the easiest parent to work with."

Sinclair turned and looked at Lori. "Ms. Summers. No one is their best self under circumstances like that."

"I guess not. Still, I'm sorry, just the same. You could have given up."

"Apology accepted. Here." Sinclair fished in the breast pocket of his uniform and produced a picture.

Three red heads with curls. Twin girls and an older sister.

"What's this?"

"This is why I didn't give up on Lana."

"Who are they?" she asked.

"They're my daughters."

"They're beautiful." She didn't know what else to say.

"Yes they are. And so is Lana." He nodded back to the room. "I think she is going to be okay. Seems like she's processing through this well. Usually stories like hers include a lot of other horrors."

"I know. Sometimes, I think I'm lucky. Other times, I'm just angry this happened at all. I don't want to think about that guy still being out there." Lori looked at her feet. "In some ways I wanted it to be Nick Rail. I wanted him to be the bad guy. It's easier to feel safe when you know the bad guy is in jail."

"I know what you mean." He gestured to the picture still in Lori's hands. And that is why I'm going to keep looking."

"How? Where do you even start with something like this?"

"Well, the only link we have is the email your daughter received. We've been working with a really good cyber detective. He knows his stuff. If anyone can turn up a lead on the perp, it will be him."

Lori handed the picture back to Sinclair.

He tucked it back in his pocket. Lori hugged the officer and watched him step into the elevator. Why couldn't Ron have been a little more like that? She wondered.

188

Sinclair threw her a wave before the doors slid closed.

Chapter 94

Nick picked up the brown envelope and flipped open the flap. Inside was his phone, and wallet. A paperclip had been placed around the cash.

He pulled on his jacket and stuffed the wallet in his jeans. He couldn't believe he was actually going home. It felt like he'd been gone forever. Lana's mother dropped off a note telling him to stop by.

Officer Sinclair opened the door and stepped into the room. "You all set?"

Nick gave him a look.

Sinclair shrugged. "How are you supposed to feel toward someone who was hunting you down, right?"

"Something like that." Nick grinned.

"Hell if I know." Sinclair shrugged. "That's how it happens sometimes."

"No hard feelings?" Sinclair offered his hand.

"No hard feelings." Nick shook the hand. "Wait. I've got something for you." Nick retrieved his wallet and pulled out a wad of cash. "Here's for that tire."

"Don't worry about it."

"Please, it will make me feel better. I won't be buying my own tires for a while anyway."

Sinclair chuckled. "Fair enough." He took the cash. "You ready to go?"

"I don't know. I was just starting to like it here."

Chapter 95

Lana Summers stepped out of the car and looked up at her own home. She wanted to talk to Nick. Had he really asked that guy to pick her up? Nothing made sense.

"Welcome home." Her mother held the front door. "I missed you."

"This feels so weird," Lana said.

"Weird how?"

"Weird because it seems like I've been away so long."

"It *was* too long. But you're home now. All that is behind us."

"Do you think I'll be able to just go back to normal. That man's still out there somewhere. I keep expecting him to walk in the door."

Lana crowded close to her mom. Lori unlocked the deadbolt and put an arm around her daughter.

"Mom, I can't believe he would just drop me off and leave me to die. Why does someone do that?"

"Stop, honey. Don't do that. Don't play that game. You aren't there anymore. Come on, let's go inside."

Chapter 96

Preston Farwick pushed through the double doors and tapped on the security glass to get the receptionist's attention. She smiled and pressed a button. The inside doors buzzed; he let himself in.

"Sinclair is waiting for you," the receptionist said.

"Great. Where's he at?"

"Right through there."

Farwick tapped on the door and pushed it open. "You ready for me?"

Sinclair dropped what he was doing and stood up. "Preston. Thanks for coming over so quickly."

"Sure. Chief Gregson plans to bill you guys pretty hard for my time. Pity I don't get a pay raise out of the deal."

Sinclair laughed and shook his hand. "Come in. Dixon told me all about you."

"Oh yeah? What'd he say?"

"Said you made the best coffee out of anyone in the office." Sinclair chuckled.

"That's only because I sneak in my own. The stuff they stock there makes hospital coffee taste good."

Sinclair motioned for a chair and sat down again. "Dixon also said you were the best guy he knew at dealing with cyber investigations."

"Very kind. But you're probably not going to like what I found."

"Which was?"

"Not much."

"Nick Rail provided the password to his email. I checked it out. The emails he received from the perp were completely untraceable. The guy obviously knew what he was doing. He must have used a high anonymity proxy. They're almost impossible to crack."

Sinclair sighed. "Shit."

"And that email sent from 'Nick' asking her to meet him over in Morris?"

"Part of that was relatively simple. The perp used his regular hide to keep his IP from showing and set up a new email account under someone else's name."

"What does that leave us?"

"More than you might think. You've got a perp who obviously knows both these kids. The guy was aware of their relationship and knew to use that against them. That narrows the playing field considerably."

"Yes, it does. But I guess I was hoping you could give me a little more."

"Well, I have a set of party dreadlocks in my closet. If you ever find this guy and want me to dress for a line up so she can ID the guy, let me know."

Sinclair laughed. "I'll keep that in mind. Thanks."

Farwick pulled Lana's laptop from his bag and set it on the table. "Here's the girl's computer, though I'm guessing she won't be too eager to get online after what she's been through."

"I agree. Pity some kids have to learn the hard way."

"True. But it's not exactly a fair playing field. They just don't know what they don't know."

Chapter 97

Nick Rail doused the lights and turned the van off the road. He ignored the 'Posted: No Trespassing' signs and followed the two-track, gravel lane back to the quarry. He crawled over bumps and skirted large potholes. No one came back here.

An ashy fog tangled in the branches of the denuded woods squatting naked around the quarry. He maneuvered the van close to the quarry's edge, killed the engine and waited, watching the lane behind him. Distant clouds hazed over a piqued moon above the hills. Nothing else.

He got out of the van and opened the rear hatch. The dome light blinked off and Nick sat on the bumper until his eyes adjusted to the dark.

He took off his coat and shivered as he pulled off his shirt and jeans. He stepped into his wetsuit, fought it up his legs and stuffed his arms into the sleeves. He grabbed the cord attached to the back zipper and pulled it up. The machine taped and glued seams would help keep some water out, but they didn't do much to improve flexibility.

Nick stood the air tank on the carpeted floor of the van and synched tight the strap holding the buoyancy control device to the tank. He cracked the tank valve to see if it was fresh and ran his finger around the mouth of the tank to make sure the O-ring was in place.

A noise brought him upright; he listened. Something rustled in the woods. Probably a rodent or owl. He turned to the tank and attached the first stage regulator, tightened the yoke screw and hooked up the low pressure inflator hose to the buoyancy control device or BCD. Air hissed into the vest at the push of a button then exhaled with another.

Nick attached the secondary regulator to the tank and made sure the octopus and pressure gauges were clipped securely to the BCD. Then he slipped a hand-held dive-light into a webbed pocket on the vest.

Nick strapped the dive computer to his left wrist and punched a button. It beeped and the lighted display threw a green glow onto the chest of his dive suit. He wasn't sure exactly how far down he would have to go. He only had his recreational, no decompression dive certificate. Not that anyone was checking out here.

The air valve on the aluminum tank squeaked as Nick turned it open before he sat on the bumper to slip into the buoyancy control vest. He tucked loose hair inside a diving hood and wiggled his hands into gloves.

An elastic band with a key dangled from his right wrist.

"Party time," Nick whispered. He grabbed his fins and mask and picked his way down the track to the water's edge. The day he killed his car seemed like another lifetime. He remembered the black bubbles and the strange wheezing noise just before it sank. Fog snarled visibility, obscuring the far quarry wall. No matter. He braced himself against the rock and pulled on his fins, securing the heel straps.

He lifted the mask over his eyes and swept his right arm around to get ahold of the regulator. He double checked the oxygen supply, tapped a button on his dive computer and frog walked into the water.

Nick finned clear of the access road that descended into the quarry, and switched on his dive light. Ice water seeped around the edges of the suit. It would warm up soon enough and help to insulate. Right now it was just cold. The shaft of light zigzagged through black water, probing the deep belly of the spring fed quarry. In spite of the darkness, the water was surprisingly clear. Crystalline, even. Only darkness outside his beam inhibited the view.

Nick adjusted the pressure in his buoyancy control device and descended slowly. He learned to dive in the Caribbean, off the coast of St. John. One of his family's regular summer vacations. Men in the oil business didn't take their families camping.

The brilliant sunshine of the Caribbean waters certainly made it easier to keep one's imagination at bay. This wasn't anything like that. Here, the panels of black surrounding him could house any number of monsters. Nick fought to keep his mind on task.

He flashed the wall and saw lines where drills made holes for dynamite. The single beam of his light reached like a cable he followed deeper into the depths.

He wondered how many guys had ever gone swimming to find their car. He smiled around the mouthpiece of his regulator. Nick followed the wall down and was rewarded to find another ledge, another road cut further down. The wide rock walls tapered in, vaguely conical in shape. The road had given access to equipment and machinery and men. The entire quarry stretched over 400 meters at the top. He had no idea how wide it was at the bottom. Hopefully, he wouldn't have to find out. The most information he could find online about the history of the quarry suggested it was well below the dive limits of his training.

A shape erupted in his path. There it was.

The car sat only twenty-feet beneath him, looking as if someone had just parked it there and stepped out to get a drink.

Nick finned toward it and panned his light across the sides. It looked perfect. Not a scratch could be seen on the near side. The wheels had turned inward toward the quarry wall, keeping the car from rolling deeper down the road. He flew over the car, watching as memories reeled across the screen of his mind. Picnic baskets, blankets and fumbled buttons. A light sediment had settled over the upholstery. The invisible water made is seem as if he could just step in and drive it away.

Not likely.

Nick checked his dive monitor then pulled the key from his forearm. He worked his way to the trunk and pushed the key into the lock. It turned. Bubbles showered up from underneath the lid, rolling up and off the metal like a fleet of jelly fish finally set free.

Nick dropped the key and reached in to lift away the carpet above the spare tire. A plastic bag floated up from the center of the rim and bumped along the truck lid before Nick's fingers caught it. He tucked the bundle under his right arm. It was roughly the size of the fruitcakes his grandmother insisted on giving them every year.

The dive computer indicated he was well within the limits of a no decompression dive, but Nick stopped every ten feet for a couple of minutes, then followed his own bubbles toward the surface. Safety first, he thought. He switched off the dive-light just before breaking the surface. The sallow moon had risen above the quarry, peering weakly down into the darkness around him.

Chapter 98

Darren Firth left swim practice with a teammate who dropped him off in Florin. Maybe this would stop the guilt that picked away at his sleep, Darren thought. Maybe he would forget the hurt on Lisa's face. Maybe.

The neon beer sign from Bubes Brewery threw a cold red light over the sidewalk. Darren pushed on toward the police station and poked the door-bell. He patted his coat pocket to make sure the CD was still there.

"What is this," the receptionist eyed him suspiciously, "some kind of class reunion?"

She wrote his name on a clipboard and cleared him through the doors. Darren turned the corner and stopped.

Ashley, Ralph and Chase sat waiting for him. "Why are you guys here?" he whispered.

Ashley shrugged. "For Lisa."

Chapter 99

Nick locked his bedroom door and set the plastic bag on his bed. He didn't need to count it.

He remembered the feel—the satisfying crack of wood on skull. The shocked look on the old woman's face as she looked at Seth standing by the front door.

He had laughed as Seth covered his eyes before Nick swung again.

Nick prized off the access panel behind the shower wall and stuffed the plastic bag inside. Out of sight. He lifted the panel and fit it back into place. Now he was free. He wouldn't have to go into the oil business. He would go to music school.

One hundred thousand dollars.

Chapter 100

Officer Dixon studied the material. The kids had done their homework. Illegally, mind you, but at least they were thorough. Ralph said they hadn't kept any copies. Said they wanted to honor the juvenile offenders' Constitutional right to privacy.

Funny, Dixon thought. He didn't remember that bit in the Constitution.

Dixon didn't exactly know how to handle it. The kids all seemed nice enough. He hated to turn it into a witch hunt when they seemed sincere. Besides, they might now have what they needed to bag this guy they called The Moderator.

It was over his head, for sure. He clicked the eject button and settled the disk into its jewel case. He'd let Preston Farwick play with this and see what he might turn up.

Chapter 101

Seth sat in a straight-backed lotus pose on his bunk, bare back to the door. The mattress lay on the floor. He pulled the short pencil from behind his ear and placed the next note on the line.

The music crawled from the cocoon of his mind, spread its wings and flew onto the wall. The thirty-eight lines had grown to create an intricate and complicated stencil.

Seth tucked the stub behind his ear, uncrossed his legs, and stood. Reaching above the top line of music, he printed two words.

For Grandma

He wet his lips and closed his eyes; he didn't need the music. The whistled flight of melody spirited into his cell. Silence fell away and lines of harmony filled his head. The bass surged underneath, lifting and enveloping the melody, pushing back the loneliness.

A note warbled and fell, chasing the base line in his mind, swooping down and resting, only to start up again like a coy dancer flirting with her partner. Seth could see Lana, see the wonder in her blue eyes, and the green grass spread beneath delicate toes. The ethereal swirl of her skirt rose as she spun away and fell again onto the grass. He could smell her ivory skin and feel the brush of her punk-black hair tangled with the silver sun.

Seth listened to the sound of her dance, and the slippery iridescent shimmer of her wedding-like veil. Things he would never know.

The song stopped at the corner where the staff ended. An incomplete composition. Seth backhanded tears from his face.

His eyelids opened to bare, square walls, the smell of urine, and the crush of silence.

Other Books by this author include

The Moderator (Book I)

Copyright © 2013 Dwight Kopp

The Zambezi Chronicles: The Contract

Copyright © 2012 Dwight Kopp

The Zambezi Chronicles: Critical Fault

Copyright © 2012 Dwight Kopp

The Zambezi Chronicles: Cover of Darkness

Copyright © 2012 Dwight Kopp

Thanks to

Doe Kopp, Martha and Jay Squaresky, Tiffani Rooney and Rachel Reilly
for their reading, edits and input,

David Curry for fielding questions about the justice system,

Officer Chris Genetti who leaves his pool open for the neighbors.

About the Author

Dwight Kopp lived (mostly) in Zambia, Africa until he was thirteen. His fondest memories include listening to the sound of elephants raiding the peanut fields as he drifted off to sleep. He now lives and writes in Lancaster County where he married the woman of his dreams. They have five (amazing) children.

https://www.facebook.com/dwightkoppbooks

dwightkopp.com

www.ingramcontent.com/pod-product-compliance
Lightning Source LLC
Chambersburg PA
CBHW051505170626
46811CB00002B/667